THE HOUSEHOLD TRAITORS

JOHN BLACKBURN

VALANCOURT BOOKS

The Household Traitors by John Blackburn
First published London: Jonathan Cape, 1971
First Valancourt Books edition 2013

Copyright © 1971 by John Blackburn

ISBN 978-1-939140-83-8 (*trade paperback*)
Also available as an electronic book

Published by Valancourt Books, Richmond, Virginia
Publisher & Editor: JAMES D. JENKINS
20th Century Series Editor: SIMON STERN, University of Toronto
http://www.valancourtbooks.com

All Valancourt Books publications are printed on acid free paper
that meets all ANSI standards for archival quality paper.

Set in Dante MT 11/13.6

THE HOUSEHOLD TRAITORS

JOHN BLACKBURN was born in 1923 in the village of Corbridge, England, the second son of a clergyman. Blackburn attended Haileybury College near London beginning in 1937, but his education was interrupted by the onset of World War II; the shadow of the war, and that of Nazi Germany, would later play a role in many of his works. He served as a radio officer during the war in the Mercantile Marine from 1942 to 1945, and resumed his education afterwards at Durham University, earning his bachelor's degree in 1949. Blackburn taught for several years after that, first in London and then in Berlin, and married Joan Mary Clift in 1950. Returning to London in 1952, he took over the management of Red Lion Books.

It was there that Blackburn began writing, and the immediate success in 1958 of his first novel, *A Scent of New-Mown Hay*, led him to take up a career as a writer full time. He and his wife also maintained an antiquarian bookstore, a secondary career that would inform some of Blackburn's work, including the bibliomystery *Blue Octavo* (1963). *A Scent of New-Mown Hay* typified the approach that would come to characterize Blackburn's twenty-eight novels, which defied easy categorization in their unique and compelling mixture of the genres of science fiction, horror, mystery, and thriller. Many of Blackburn's best novels came in the late 1960s and early 1970s, with a string of successes that included the classics *A Ring of Roses* (1965), *Children of the Night* (1966), *Nothing but the Night* (1968; adapted for a 1973 film starring Christopher Lee and Peter Cushing), *Devil Daddy* (1972) and *Our Lady of Pain* (1974). Somewhat unusually for a popular horror writer, Blackburn's novels were not only successful with the reading public but also won widespread critical acclaim: the *Times Literary Supplement* declared him 'today's master of horror' and compared him with the Grimm Brothers, while the *Penguin Encyclopedia of Horror and the Supernatural* regarded him as 'certainly the best British novelist in his field' and the *St James Guide to Crime & Mystery Writers* called him 'one of England's best practicing novelists in the tradition of the thriller novel'.

By the time Blackburn published his final novel in 1985, much of his work was already out of print, an inexplicable neglect that continued until Valancourt began republishing his novels in 2013. John Blackburn died in 1993.

By John Blackburn

A Scent of New-Mown Hay (1958)*
A Sour Apple Tree (1958)
Broken Boy (1959)*
Dead Man Running (1960)
The Gaunt Woman (1962)
Blue Octavo (1963)*
Colonel Bogus (1964)
The Winds of Midnight (1964)
A Ring of Roses (1965)
Children of the Night (1966)
The Flame and the Wind (1967)*
Nothing but the Night (1968)*
The Young Man from Lima (1968)
Bury Him Darkly (1969)*
Blow the House Down (1970)
The Household Traitors (1971)*
Devil Daddy (1972)
For Fear of Little Men (1972)
Deep Among the Dead Men (1973)
Our Lady of Pain (1974)*
Mister Brown's Bodies (1975)
The Face of the Lion (1976)*
The Cyclops Goblet (1977)*
Dead Man's Handle (1978)
The Sins of the Father (1979)
A Beastly Business (1982)*
The Book of the Dead (1984)
The Bad Penny (1985)*

* Available or forthcoming from Valancourt Books

Preface

'Walk to the dunes – crawl to the wood – then, run for it.' Those had been his instructions and Alban came running.

He was through the wood at last. The stunted pine trees, bent inland by the prevailing wind from the sea, had given way to shrub, and beyond the shrub lay the open heath without a trace of cover. There was still a long way to go, and though he'd been told that it would be easy, he hadn't realized how out of condition he was. Alban's feet slipped and stumbled through the thick grass and bracken, his whole body shuddered with the effort and there appeared to be blood instead of saliva in his mouth. But somehow he forced himself to keep pounding on through the mist he had prayed for. Surely its joint odours of salt and seaweed must confuse the dogs and give him a chance?

No, they had the scent. The fence and the road in front still looked immensely far off, while behind him the confused sounds of the chase had united into a single peal of excitement. Freedom might lie ahead, but the hunters were coming in for the kill; armed men and dogs against one tired animal.

Less than two hundred yards now. The mist was thinning and he could see the individual rails of the fence quite clearly. Beyond them lay the cutting and the road where help would be waiting. If they didn't release the dogs – if he was given that one mercy, he might just make it.

A hundred yards; surely no farther than that? He swerved to avoid a grazing sheep and two grouse rose screaming before him with shrill warnings of 'Go back . . . Go back . . . Go back.' He glanced over his shoulder and what he saw urged him on like a whip. At the edge of the wood the mist had lifted and three low shapes were rippling over the ground. The dogs were free and Alban had been savaged before. In spite of the taste in his mouth and the pain that racked his heart and lungs, the memory of those teeth kept him running.

Only a few more yards, and as he had been promised the gate in the fence was open. He half-ran, half-staggered towards it and paused as he saw the car parked in the lay-by below him. Then his legs gave way and he tobogganed head first down the cutting and lay gasping on the tarmac till friendly hands helped him up.

'Good boy,' said his rescuer as he let in the clutch and sent the car hurtling away to freedom. 'You made it all right, and almost dead on time, eh, Hangman?'

Chapter One

'Forty-eight hours have passed and the police have no more information regarding the escape of Harry Alban from Seamont open prison.' George Grant, junior partner of Allied Concessions, stared at the heavy, nondescript face glowing on the television screen.

'Up to last January, Alban, who was convicted of murdering three women by strangulation with a necktie and is known as the Mad Hangman, had been serving his life sentence at the Brondincoombe top-security institution for the criminally insane. But as he was considered to be responding to psychiatric treatment, the Home Secretary authorized his transfer to Seamont.' The murderer's picture was replaced by a rambling Georgian mansion surrounded by pine woods and with a view of the sea behind them.

'How Alban managed to make his getaway remains a mystery.' The second picture faded and the announcer reappeared. 'It seems unlikely that a man of his type would have associates prepared to organize the escape and the police consider that he must be hiding out in the Seamont area and will be arrested before long. Dr Albert Cox, the resident psychiatrist at the prison, has stated that in his professional opinion Alban is no longer dangerous, but members of the public are warned not to approach him . . .

'The Lauder Valley controversy remains a cause for concern. Gordon Rammage reports.' Another news item was beginning and the screen revealed first a river winding through pasture land, and then a village square dominated by a church.

George Grant sighed as he pulled at his pipe. He was a heavily built man in his mid-thirties with a beard which was already turning grey and mild, brown eyes which contrasted with a craggy face.

'What is the future of this village?' The reporter was seen walking away from the church towards a bridge. 'Once a prosperous residential area and a world-famous beauty spot, Laudervale is rapidly becoming a ghost town, and the reason is easy to find.' The camera zoomed to show that the river was polluted and steam was rising from a blanket of scummy foam.

'Since Allied Concessions opened their synthetic dye and plastics factory three miles upstream from here, property values are dwindling and local hotel keepers report that their tourist trade is at a standstill. Though questions have been asked in both Houses of Parliament and a nation-wide petition organized to preserve the valley's amenities, it seems clear that Allied Concessions were given full planning permission and are within their legal rights.' A line of chimneys belching smoke appeared on the horizon and George switched off the set.

'Yes, our legal rights are in order; they always are, Boris.' He grimaced at the man slumped in a chair before him. They had been checking the details of a contract and had just finished before the news. 'Those chimneys will go on smoking and the river run foul till Sir Ernest Grant, K.C.M.G., your employer and my father, tells them to stop. How do you like working for us?'

'Rather an unfair question for the boss's son to ask me.' Boris Orel, one of the firm's advisers on Iron Curtain markets, smiled back at him.

'I am a refugee, a Russian defector who asked your government for political asylum. I am grateful to them for a passport and to Allied for a job.' Boris followed George's stare towards an oil painting of the chairman. He had only met Sir Ernest Grant briefly on one occasion, and since his wife's death in a motor accident and the stroke that had followed it the old man had become something of a recluse. But during that short interview he had sensed a little of the arrogance that the artist had hinted at in the picture. The stroke might have slowed him down, but Grant still controlled his empire with an iron hand and behind his back was referred to as Deadly Earnest. His close associates appeared to regard him with something akin to awe and the portrait suggested that they were right. The eyes that stared from the painted features looked as if they would only smile at a rival's misfortune.

'Yes, I'm happy enough here,' Boris said. 'My former masters were quite as ruthless as your father is said to be and I enjoy driving a hard bargain with them from time to time.

'Thank you. Two fingers and plenty of soda.' Boris nodded at George's offer of a drink, feeling rather proud of his acquired English idiom. It was nearly two years since he had asked for sanctuary in the West and he had come to regard England as his home already. At times he could almost imagine that he had been born there.

Just under two years, but a lifetime, he thought while George mixed their drinks. His escape had been so sudden, so miraculous that much of it was blurred in his mind, though some of the details remained horribly clear. The door closing to lock him in the rear compartment, the steady gush of oil from the broken pipe and the deck of the aircraft swinging and bucking as it hurtled down without a rudder to guide it. Then there had been a sudden jolt that threw him sideways, the fuselage had opened as though a knife had ripped through it and his body was sucked out by the slipstream.

The airliner had been only two hundred feet from the ground at that moment, but his fall felt like an eternity. Faces flashed past him on the way down: his father, Shura and Tania, and Sophie, Peter Vanin and Colonel Malendin. They were all smiling as they watched his end till a great gout of flame and the roar of the explosion told him that his companions had died before him and darkness closed in.

Light must have returned very quickly, but it took him some time to know that he was still alive and even longer to realize that he was not lying in bed with a white sheet spread around him. Then full consciousness had returned and he had climbed out of the snowdrift which had saved his life and tried to gather his thoughts together. He had fallen in a park: the lights of Berlin were all around him, but at first he had no idea if he was in the East or West sector of the city. Then he saw the radio tower which had torn open the plane and it gave him his bearings. He had walked off to find a police post, but before he did, a building with a sentry at the gate and a Union Jack on the roof came into sight.

'I am a Soviet citizen . . . a survivor from that crash.' The flames from the burning aircraft were still visible as he approached the sentry and made the most important decision of his life. 'My name is Orel . . . Boris Stephanovich Orel . . . I wish to ask for political asylum in the West.'

'Stop daydreaming, old boy.' George Grant's voice interrupted his memories and he handed him the whisky and soda. 'Now, come and look at our latest asset. I think she's rather lovely.'

'Extremely so.' Boris followed him across to the opposite wall which was devoted to George's passion in life: the Port Olwyn and Bryncir Railway in North Wales. Maps of the system were displayed, there were prints of Victorian workings and photographs of stations and rolling stock and other features of the line. The most recent photograph was in colour and showed a steam locomotive in the process of restoration.

'Beautiful and raffish, like a very young street walker.' Boris's father had been an engine driver on the run between Archangel and Leningrad and he shared George's enthusiasm for early railways. That was why their business acquaintanceship had started to ripen into friendship, and he smiled affectionately at the old 2-4-0 in the photograph. She was small by twentieth-century standards and a dwarf compared to the gigantic Russian locomotives he had often ridden on when he was a boy. But she was gleaming with apple-green paint and brasswork, and a high cab, outside cylinders and tall chimney gave a fine suggestion of speed and power. Two nameplates in English and Welsh proclaimed that she was *Cambrian Rose*.

'Certainly not young, Boris. The old girl was completed in 1872 and worked for over half a century.' There was a gleam in George Grant's eyes. The Port Olwyn Railway had been abandoned after the war and lain rusting till he and a group of fellow enthusiasts had bought the bankrupt property and started to restore it. Ten miles of the original seventeen had already been opened for traffic during the summer, but the area had few other tourist attractions and Boris had heard that the project was still sucking up money like a sponge.

'*Rose* was in a terrible state when we began work on her. The motion rusted solid and grass growing in the firebox. But rebuilding is almost complete at last. I had the boiler tubes specially made at our Castle Landon works.' George gave a wry smile. 'To my father's extreme annoyance, I may say.'

'Sir Ernest does not share your enthusiasm for early railways, then?' Boris was looking at the tiny terminus of the reopened line. George had converted the station master's quarters into a weekend cottage and spent much of his free time there. 'That must be rather sad for you. It was my father who aroused my interest in them.'

'You were lucky, Boris. It must have been pleasant to share something with one's parents.' George spoke with a trace of bitterness. 'I never had much in common with mine; though that's quite natural, of course. After all, I was adopted. Didn't you know that? I thought it was common knowledge throughout the firm.' He looked at Boris's glass which was still half full and carried his own back to the table and topped it up.

'Yes, the old boy wanted a son and heir and my mother – his wife I should say, of course – couldn't or wouldn't give him one. Therefore I was procured at the late age of six. Probably he didn't want to risk taking on a young child who might have turned out to be sickly.' George flexed his right arm with a grin and took another swig of whisky.

'I am afraid we have disappointed each other. Before his stroke my father's whole life was motivated by power and money, while I'm an adequate, but hardly a dedicated businessman. I wanted his affection and till recently believed he was quite incapable of giving or receiving it.' George crossed back to the railway display, thinking of his boyhood. He had wanted far more than normal affection. He had worshipped his adopted father and craved for his love, but Sir Ernest had always remained aloof.

'I will try to look at your toys later, George, but I am very busy at the moment. So run along to Nurse and please don't bother your mother. You know how bad her nerves are.'

'What: only fifth in your class, George?' He could still hear the precise voice and the rustle of the school report. 'That is not good enough for a future director of Allied Concessions, my boy, and I will arrange that you spend the summer holidays with a tutor.'

'You said, "till recently he was incapable of love"?' Boris hesitated before asking a question. Though George Grant appeared to regard him as a friend, he was only a fairly junior employee talking to the son of the chairman. 'Has your father mellowed since his illness?'

'I had hoped so, Boris. He and my mother were not on affectionate terms, but her death shook him up badly and probably caused his stroke. Then when he came out of hospital he did seem to want to establish a closer relationship with me. We often dined together and he even tried to show an interest in the railway and my two charitable activities. I run a boys' club near the docks and do a bit of prison visiting.' George looked towards the window. Allied's head office was the tallest building in the city of Daneville and the big, grimy town lay spread out beneath them. To the west the river wound its way towards the Irish Sea, and to the north clouds shrouded the hills, heralding rain.

'Yes, for a few months I really thought that even Deadly Earnest needed somebody's love, but I was quite wrong.' For the second time Boris noted the bitterness in his voice. 'My father by adoption was not looking for normal human affection. What he hopes to find is a phantom; a dream that has festered in a very disturbed mind indeed.' There was a knock on the door and George turned as his secretary came in with the evening paper.

'Ah, Miss Robbins. Take these along to "Files" please and then you may go.' He held out the contract. 'I won't need you any more today.'

'Thank you, sir.' She took the folder from him and turned to go. 'To tell you the truth I won't be sorry to get home early tonight: and put the chain on the door too. Seamont's only forty miles from here and no woman's going to be safe till they catch that maniac.' She gave a mock shiver and hurried back into the outer office.

'Silly little fool.' George looked down at the front page of the paper. Questions regarding prison security had been asked in the Lords and the Seamont escape was still news. Alban's heavy face was prominently displayed and beneath it lay the faces of his victims: three middle-aged women. 'Uninformed fear of the mentally ill is so childish. So dangerous, too. Ethel Robbins is a pleasant, kindly girl, but that's the kind of attitude which causes pogroms.'

'Surely she has some reason for anxiety?' Boris had crossed over beside him. 'The doctors may say that this man was responding to treatment, but after all he has killed three people. Doesn't the escape itself prove he's still a public danger?'

'Why should it? Have you ever been inside a prison, Boris?'

'As a matter of fact, I have.' Memory stabbed at his brain like a needle. 'But not a British prison.'

'What's the difference? They are all places of confinement and a craving for freedom is a basic human emotion. And whatever these people may have done, they are human beings with souls.' George was warming to a cause that concerned him deeply. 'Seamont is one of the three prisons I visit, as it happens, and I've talked to some of the worst cases there, including Harry Alban. If one could only find the pressure behind them, the motivation that drove them to crime, they could all be cured and become ordinary, useful citizens.'

'But surely they have to be locked up till they are cured?' Boris had never seen George so passionate. 'You can't have criminal lunatics walking about as free as air. Shouldn't the potential victims be considered?'

'You sound like my father.' Boris's glass was empty now and George refilled it and his own. 'If he had his way, not only the gallows, but the cat-o'-nine-tails and the stocks would be back in operation. I've even heard him advocate mutilation for sexual offenders. No, understanding is the only way to deal with the problem, Boris. And though I'm not a very religious man, I believe that "Father, forgive them; for they know not what they do" is the greatest text there is.

'George Grant here.' The telephone had rung and he picked it up. 'Hullo Michael, what can I do for you? Yes, Orel's with me now. Should I put him on to you?' All passion had left him and George looked puzzled. 'Very well, I'll give him the message.

'How very strange.' He frowned at Boris while he lowered the instrument into its rest. 'You don't have any dealings with my father, do you?'

'I've only met him once.' Boris was frowning back at him. 'Most probably I'm only a name on the payroll to him.'

'Apparently you're wrong. Michael Byrne, his secretary, says that you're to go over to his house. He told Byrne that it was a personal matter.' George's pipe had gone out and he started to refill it.

'Something personal and he hardly knows you. What the hell can he be up to? All rather disturbing. As I said, I've been worried about his health recently. Be a good chap and let me know what he wants, Boris. In return I'll give you a piece of advice.' George broke off and lit the pipe with agonizing slowness.

'My father is an old, tired man, but he's still an autocrat who likes to control people; to own them body, soul and mind, if they'll give him the chance. So don't allow him to bully you.' He reached out and took Boris's hand in a friendly grasp.

'There's a proverb about using a long spoon when you sup with the devil and he's a devil, all right.'

Chapter Two

'You still consider that Salinger-Brown will refuse our second offer, Michael? Let me have the facts as you see them, please.' Sir Ernest Grant stood by the window of his study while his secretary went through the day's reports with him. His house lay high on the fells above Daneville and while he listened he looked at the things he owned and had made. The lights of the Allied Building towering up into the evening sky, the glow of blast furnaces on the far horizon, the big freighter, *Daneville Argus* nosing its way through the canal.

'Yes, you're probably right in thinking that the board won't budge for eleven and sixpence a share, even though we and our nominees own thirty-two per cent of the voting stock. Peter Brown is a stubborn fellow, and I have the greatest respect for him. On the surface our offer looks attractive, but as we both know, Salinger's frozen assets are very considerable.' Though the weather was mild and the heating was on, Ernest Grant had never felt really warm since his stroke six months ago and he massaged his hands together while he talked.

'But a little bird told me that Peter is also a sick fellow, Michael. Gallstone trouble and very painful, poor chap. He's going to need surgery soon, so we'd better play a waiting game. Then, when he's safely in hospital, increase the bid to twelve shillings. Without Peter to stop them the other directors will accept without a murmur. Now, how is the French charter business progressing?' Tugs were edging the freighter into the docks now. Soon she would start to unload wheat and wood pulp from Canada and take on machine tools from the new plant outside Leeds. The containers carrying those machine tools would be transported by Allied's lorries and travel along the motorway that its subsidiary company Daneville Construction had helped to build.

'They complain that the rates are too high by five per cent, eh? Which means that Martin Whitecross is not such a good salesman as we supposed.' Sir Ernest felt personal failure as he said that because he prided himself on his selection of employees. 'Say we'll come down by two and a half and sack Whitecross first thing in the morning.' On a table in the centre of the room a buzzer whirred and he waited for Byrne to answer the intercom.

'Good.' He looked at his watch and nodded. 'Orel has got here promptly, so I won't keep him waiting. Go down for him please, Michael, but don't bother to come back yourself. Just show him the way and tell him to come straight in without knocking.' Grant did not move when his secretary had left him. His eyes were fixed towards the glowing stream of the motorway and behind them he could see his wife's face clearly. Madge driving across the Pennines and driving exactly as fast as a Bentley could be driven. Poor Madge; they'd known each other since they were children, he'd been fond of her in a way, but he had never managed to return her love. That was why she drank so much, of course. They had found a lot of alcohol in what was left of her body and there was a flask of brandy on the seat beside her. Had she reached out for the flask just before the car went out of control, he wondered? Had she had her last drink before she died? He hoped so, because he wouldn't have liked Madge to have died thirsty. Behind him the door opened and closed, but Grant still didn't move. Brandy had killed Madge in the end, and she had started to drink when she realized he could never love her. Madge was one more ghost to trouble his conscience.

'Sir Ernest.' Boris had been standing silently for a full thirty seconds before he spoke, looking at the motionless figure by the window and glancing around the room. Ernest Grant was very tall and as bulky as George and his shoulders were as straight as a guardsman's. His study was large and gloomy with heavy mahogany furniture, and a faded grey carpet covered the floor. Shelves of leather-bound books filled one wall and to the right of the doorway stood a marble bust of its owner. A desk bearing three telephones and the intercom, and a line of filing cabinets beside it were the only things associated with big business. From what Boris had seen, the rest of the house was bright and tasteful; probably the late Lady Grant had been responsible for that, but this was the room of a man to whom his surroundings were supremely unimportant. 'Mr Byrne told me to come straight up, sir.'

'Good evening, Mr Orel.' At last Grant turned and Boris saw that he had been wrong in thinking of him as a guardsman. He might be tall and well built, his shoulders and back might be straight, but the aura of the man coming slowly across the room to greet him was not that of a soldier, but of a clergyman.

'It is good of you to get here so quickly.' Grant's handshake was hard and dry and his voice rather attractive. Like his expression it gave no hint of his feelings; a well-tuned instrument designed to convey information, but never emotion.

'There are drinks over there if you require one, Mr Orel. I do not indulge myself, but have no objection to others doing so.' He nodded towards a sideboard, but Boris shook his head. He was completely baffled by the summons and wanted to keep his head clear. 'No thank you, sir. I had a drink with your son earlier on, as it happens.'

'Yes, I understand that Mr Byrne located you in George's office. George drinks rather heavily, I am sorry to say. But do sit down and make yourself comfortable.' Grant waved him to a chair and took three cardboard folders from the filing cabinet.

'I've been given good reports about your progress with us, Mr Orel.' He laid down the folders on his desk and switched on an Anglepoise lamp. The beam was directed straight at Boris's eyes and he felt far from comfortable. He felt exactly as he had done during his last security check before leaving Russia.

'It is a pity that as a defector you cannot travel behind the Iron Curtain or deal directly with any of our Eastern associates, but you are doing most valuable work in the office. We may have to think about promotion one day, but before that happens I want you to understand something.' The old man paused for a moment, studying Boris's face under the lamp. 'The two things I demand from my senior executives are complete loyalty and the willingness to undertake duties which may sometimes seem to be outside their normal field of employment. Is that quite clear?'

'Perfectly, sir.' Boris was very much on his guard, because he had heard similar statements so many times before. 'The Party demands unswerving obedience, comrade. During your visit to the Kirov bicycle factory you will discover whether the works manager, Igor Skrydloff, is as politically reliable as he appears.' He suspected that Sir Ernest was about to question him on the efficiency of the marketing department, as Grant had some reason to do. Boris's superior, Dr Tyrel, was an elderly man and there was no denying that he took things pretty easily. All the same he was very fond of old Bill Tyrel and he was damned if he would say a word against him.

'Good.' The first part of the security check was over and Grant sat down and tilted the lamp over the top folder. There was the hint of a smile on his lips as he opened it and glanced at the contents.

'You'll know this by heart, Mr Orel. The account of your life in Russia, as told by yourself.' He put on his glasses to read the typescript. Behind them his sharp eyes looked much milder and his whole face less formidable.

'You were born at Archangel in nineteen thirty-four . . . . father a locomotive engineer . . . mother vanished during the war; probably taken to Germany as a slave labourer. Tch, tch.' Grant's tongue clicked sympathetically. 'Graduated from Moscow University, with a degree in economic history . . . Proficiency in three foreign languages, English, German and Spanish . . . unmarried . . . position held before your defection to the West was that of consultant in commercial economics.

'All very commendable, but there is something even more important in your favour. Napoleon once queried a general's appointment because he was unlucky, and you appear to be a very lucky man.' In the painting in George's office, Grant's eyes had looked as though they would rarely smile, but Boris saw them twinkle behind the glasses as they registered his own expression.

'Surely you don't deny that, Mr Orel? You were a member of a trade mission travelling from Moscow to East Germany in a TL19 airliner. For some unknown reason the aircraft went out of control while it was off course and crashed in a suburb of West Berlin. You were the only survivor out of a party of thirty-three because you happened to be in the rear baggage section which struck the mast of the *Funkturm* in West Berlin. All your companions were killed when the plane hit the ground, but you were sucked out through the damaged fuselage and had the very good fortune to fall into a deep snowdrift. Quite providential that you were in that rear section of the plane, Mr Orel. You should thank your Maker for such an escape.'

'I was standing in the aisle talking to a friend when the aircraft went out of control.' Sir Ernest's manner had been perfectly friendly, but Boris had tensed as if an inborn warning device was flashing a danger signal. The British and German intelligence officers had accepted his story without question, but he had a feeling that Grant was sceptical. 'The sudden lurch threw me back through the hatch.'

'Which happened to be open. Yes, Dame Fortune smiled on you that day.' Sir Ernest might have been complimenting him on some personal achievement. 'Thirty-two most probably loyal Soviet citizens die, but the one man with a wish to defect survives and walks into the British military barracks at Spandau.

'Intelligence, academic qualifications, the capacity for hard work.' He eyed Tyrel's comments on a page. 'Also luck. We are most fortunate to have obtained your services. Now, about the reason I sent for you. The special mission outside your normal duties.' The old man was sucking a throat tablet and a tang of menthol drifted from his lips. 'The fact is that since my wife died I have been lonely; hellishly lonely.'

'I'm sorry.' There was nothing else to say, but Boris could not have been more astonished if Grant had suddenly sacked him or offered him a seat on the board.

'Does that surprise you very much, Mr Orel?' Sir Ernest closed the first folder and opened the second. 'Office gossip must have told you that I did not love my wife and married her for money; though that is not quite true. It was power, not money I wanted. Madge had been infatuated with me since we were children and her father was chairman of the company. He thought we would make a go of things in time and promised me a directorship if I married her. No, I never loved Madge, Mr Orel, but I don't love this either.' He laid his right hand on the desk. 'All the same, I would feel a loss if it were amputated.'

'It is perfectly natural that you should miss your wife, sir.' Boris frowned at him in complete bewilderment. 'But I find it very strange that you should discuss your personal feelings with me.'

'You'll understand soon enough and I'm afraid it's not a very pleasant story.' Grant took a photograph from the file, held it under the light for an instant and then pushed it across to Boris. 'Do you find her attractive?'

'She is very pretty indeed.' The photograph showed a girl in her late teens or early twenties; she had fair hair and her features were small and rather elf-like. She was smiling towards the camera, but though the face was almost beautiful, there was a certain hardness about the mouth and eyes. Across the foot of the photograph was written 'To my darling Ernest from his Paddy, ITALY.'

'The picture was not taken abroad, but during a day trip to Brighton in the nineteen thirties, Mr Orel.' Sir Ernest eased back his chair. 'The letters contained in ITALY denote I THALL ALWAYS LOVE YOU. Arch, sickly, childish, you may think, but Paddy was a child when she wrote it. I am now going to tell you about her, and please smoke if you want to.' He moved across to the window again and stood with his back towards Boris while he told his story.

Ernest Grant was a young man attached to Allied's London office when he met the girl at a party. Her name was Patricia Reilly and she was a student from a town not far from Daneville where Grant was born. That started their friendship and after discussing their mutual backgrounds they began to think it possible that there might be some distant family connection through the female lines.

Be that as it may, they became lovers and lived together for just over a year till the chairman of Allied Concessions made his offer and pointed out the strings attached to it. 'I'm retiring soon, my boy, but I want to keep control in the family. Buy a house up here, marry Madge, and I'll see that you step into my shoes before too long. Love? Don't worry about that, son. Madge is devoted to you and you'll feel the same towards her in time. Remember what Lady Disraeli said: "Dizzy may have married me for money, but he'd marry me for love now." Think things over, Ernest, and let me have your agreement within a week.'

It hadn't taken Ernest Grant anything like a week to make up his mind. He might have loved Paddy, but he loved power more. Almost before he lowered the telephone he had decided to accept.

'So you left the girl?' Grant had fallen silent and Boris prompted him. George was right, he thought. The old man was mentally sick, and if it had not been for the photograph he might have dismissed the story as imaginary. 'That still distresses you after such a long time, sir?'

'Yes, Orel, because I did more than just leave her. Paddy knew that Madge was a strait-laced woman who would never have married me if there was any chance of a scandal. She threatened to tell Madge all about our affair and turn up at the church when the banns were read. She said that she'd ruin me. So I beat Paddy up, Orel. I only intended to frighten her off, but I lost control of myself completely. I think I might have killed her if the neighbours hadn't intervened. I scarred her face with this.' His right hand jerked back and Boris saw a signet ring glint on the index finger. 'But I succeeded in frightening her all right. Paddy kept quiet and six months later Madge and I were married. What a fool I was.' He paused and shrugged his shoulders before continuing the story.

Unlike Disraeli, Grant never learned to love his wife and their relationship was a marriage in name only. Five years later he met Miss Reilly by chance in a London restaurant and at first glance realized that he still loved her. He had begged her to forgive him and offered her money and security if she would become his mistress again, but the woman had listened in silence and then pointed to a scar on her cheek and thrown a cup of coffee into his face.

'She was a strange person, Orel. I don't think it was only fear that stopped her making trouble for me. Even if I hadn't hit her, her pride would have made her keep quiet. So proud and so bitter she was. I was a rich man when I met her again. I could have given her so much, but she still hadn't forgiven me after all those years. Can you understand a woman preserving really deep hatred for so long?'

'Yes, Sir Ernest. Women can be very dedicated haters.' Boris studied the photograph again. The girl's eyes and mouth were not merely hard, they looked cruel, too. 'But what I can't understand is why you should confide in me. We hardly know each other.'

'It's quite simple, my boy. We'll know each other better before long and I need your help.' Grant left the window and returned to the desk. His body was as erect as ever but his feet dragged on the carpet. 'As I told you, I felt lonely after Madge was killed and then I had that stroke. The physical pain was like being stabbed, but when the pain stopped I was in a sort of semi-coma and I started to understand things. I heard a song on the radio and I kept seeing Paddy's face all the time. It was like having a vision, Orel, and it told me that my whole life had been wasted because power and money are nothing compared to love and I really had worshipped Paddy.' He reached out and turned the photograph towards him and Boris saw that there was a hint of tears in his eyes.

'So, when I got back to normal I decided to find her again. She's not dead and she didn't marry, as far as I know, so when I find her, I'm going to try and put things right. To beg her forgiveness and ask her to become my wife. I started to look for Paddy about a month ago. First I advertised in the press and then hired a private detective; a local man called Paulson who practises here in Daneville. He dropped the case and went abroad as it happens, but all the information he got hold of is in here.' Grant tapped the second folder. His voice had been faltering and almost inaudible for some time, but now it was as precise as before. 'There is not a great deal, but it will give you something to start on.'

'I still don't understand you.' Bewilderment was clouding Boris's thoughts, but another emotion had started to join it. 'You want me to find the woman?'

'Exactly, Orel. And when you find her, your salary will be increased by fifty per cent and you will get Dr Tyrel's job when he retires next January. That's not a bad offer, my boy, so is it a deal?'

'No, because I don't happen to be a detective, Sir Ernest.' Bewilderment was drifting away and the second emotion had grown stronger and stronger. It was fear, and Boris recalled George's proverb of the devil and the long spoon. 'You may expect your staff to undertake extra duties, but surely not those quite outside their experience.'

'You are being too modest, Orel.' Grant was opening the third folder. 'I have studied your career with interest and I am quite sure that you are the person who can find Paddy for me.' He took out a magazine and laid it under the lamp. 'I read Russian and I make a point of consulting Soviet technical journals. The other day I was going through this back number and I happened to come across a certain item that puzzled me more than a little.' His hand flicked through the pages. 'Mr Tchagin, the Soviet trade attaché over here is a very good friend of mine; we often lunch or dine together when I am in London, and because an illustration in this article was so puzzling I sought his help.' There were no tears in Sir Ernest's eyes now and they looked as cold as glass beads that had been screwed into his face by some repulsive surgical operation. 'Alexis Tchagin was most informative, but a few loose ends remain and I wonder if you can help me.' He pushed the magazine across to Boris and leaned back.

'You devil. God, you old devil.' Boris's heart was thumping

against his ribs and he spoke in gasps. The page contained nineteen photographs. Each showed the face of a man or a woman and each had a name beneath it. He had known them all; some of his fellow members on the doomed trade mission.

'Maybe I am a devil, but you're a curious fellow, my boy, because one face and one name do not appear to match each other.' Deadly Earnest gave a mirthless chuckle. '"The voice is Jacob's voice, but the hands are the hands of Esau."'

'So, have we a deal, Orel? Are you going to look for Paddy or must I talk to Mr Tchagin again?' He watched Boris clench his fists and knew that at that moment his one ambition in life was to kill him. But he was also quite sure that reason would prevail, and he was right. After a time the hands opened and Boris nodded. The deal was on.

Chapter Three

'He can ruin you, Boris Stephanovich. Grant can snap you and Shura and Tania between his fingers.' Boris muttered aloud in the sitting-room of his flat, scowling down at Aly's (as the firm was often called) annual report to its shareholders. He had been studying the brochure the previous evening and it was open to show a photograph of Sir Ernest above the chairman's report, while on the opposite page visible proofs of progress were displayed. These included a new type of diesel locomotive, and as he looked at it Boris thought of the steam locomotives of his youth. The cantankerous Pacific his father called 'Ivan the Terrible' snorting through the pine forests, and his sense of excitement and freedom rising with the piston beats while the speed increased and the pine trees went rushing past.

Freedom! The dream he had heard Ivan Golikov proclaim on the aircraft's address system while Radek's gun had bored into the back of his neck. 'We are taking this plane to freedom and in a few minutes you will be landing at Gatow aerodrome in West Berlin. Those of you who believe in liberty may join us in asking the German authorities for sanctuary. But whatever your feelings, you must all remain in your seats and keep calm. The crew have promised to collaborate and resistance is impossible.'

'Come with me, comrade. I know what you are, so stand up very slowly.' Radek had kept the muzzle against him as he obeyed. 'No, leave your jacket and walk back down the aisle. I am locking you in the baggage compartment till we have landed.' Step by step he had edged him on towards the rear door and then motioned him through.

Boris still did not know what had prompted him to resist. He regarded Ivan Golikov as a friend, and he sympathized with his and Radek's desire to defect; if he had been a single man he might have joined them. But he had Shura and Tania to think of and his failure to stop the hijacking might affect them as much as himself. Also he had been trained to obey since boyhood. After he had stepped back through the hatch, he had seen that Radek's hand was against the frame and he had kicked out in an almost reflex action, slamming the heavy door home across his wrist. Then, just as automatically, Radek had fired, the bullet had shattered the rudder control line and the aircraft had gone plummeting down towards liberty for himself and death for his companions.

A short-lived spell of liberty, however. Only two years had passed and the chains were around him again.

'Your motives for defecting under the name of a man who died in the crash are no concern of mine,' Sir Ernest Grant had said. 'All that concerns me is that you are a man with the qualifications to carry out the assignment I have set you. Yes, Alexis Tchagin drinks rather a lot and he was most forthcoming, Orel.' He stressed the name slightly. 'I gathered that you are a person whom the Soviet government would like to recover and that they have the means to do so. If you were alive, naturally. I also gathered that you are of a ruthless disposition and I am sure you would not hesitate to kill me. Let me advise you to do nothing of the kind.'

Grant had spoken with complete assurance. 'The information regarding you is lodged in my bank with orders to make it public knowledge if I should die violently. So, just do what I say and you will have nothing to worry about. Tchagin has not the slightest notion that you exist. He merely thought that I was pumping him out of idle curiosity. Find Miss Reilly for me and you will be rewarded with promotion. Fail and I imagine you will have to board another airliner. One going back to the Soviet Union this time. Now, get to work.'

He had closed the folder and handed it to Boris. 'All the information I can give you is in here and you have indefinite leave of absence from the office. Good night, Orel. I shall expect you to report your progress to me at regular intervals.' He had given a curt nod and walked back to the window. The interview was over.

To find a woman who had not been heard of for over thirty years. That could be one hell of a job, and even if he did find her, would Grant honour his promise of silence? Probably, because Deadly Earnest would not want to lose a valuable slave whom he owned like any other piece of property. Boris poured himself another vodka: his third since he had come back to the flat and stared through the window. The lights of an aircraft were heading east across the city and he shivered slightly as he watched them. If Sir Ernest did keep his word, would his life be worth anything? He had merely exchanged one form of slavery for another and Grant was astride his neck like the Old Man of the Sea. If Grant ever informed against him he would receive a summons to return home and have to obey it. Boris opened the window and leaned out over the sill. The street was eight storeys beneath him and at the end of that drop lay peace and freedom. There were many worse ways to die. Nobody knew that better than he did.

He would not die yet, though. Boris drew back and returned to the desk. He hated and feared Ernest Grant as much as any human being he had known, but he was also very curious about him. The radio was playing old-time dance music with the volume turned low and a waltz tune made him consider the sentimental side of Grant's nature. A ruthless man who could use blackmail to gain his ends, but who was also tortured by guilt and the craving to be reunited with a woman he had ill-treated thirty-six years ago.

A woman who probably still loathed him, if she was alive. The contents of the file were spread out on his desk and Boris looked at Grant's early attempt to locate Miss Reilly: a small 'ad' that had been inserted in all the major newspapers: 'Paddy, please contact E.G. who still loves you.' Beside the clipping was a typewritten reply which had been posted from a town in Northumberland. 'E.G. Leave me alone. Paddy.' That could mean nothing, of course. People of cruel and perverse humour do answer such advertisements as a joke, and the note might have been sent by a hoaxer. All the same, it had convinced Grant that Miss Reilly was alive and he had employed the private detective Eric Paulson to locate her, agreeing to pay him five thousand pounds if he was successful. Paulson's reports were contained in the file, and Sir Ernest had covered six foolscap pages with every fact he imagined could help. Boris sat down to study the data.

Paulson had appeared confident of earning his handsome fee at first. Official records suggested that Miss Reilly was alive and unmarried, but might have changed her name. Still full of confidence he had chased about the country following various possibilities with enthusiasm, and then quite suddenly had thrown in his hand. His final letter stated that the task was proving fruitless and he believed that the woman was most probably dead. He had one more lead to explore, and if that came to nothing, he had decided to drop the case and accept another which entailed his leaving the country for some weeks.

That was the last that Grant had heard from Paulson. He had called at the office to find that it was locked up, and the janitor had no information for him. Clearly the detective had left town on other business.

Lucky Paulson, Boris thought, pulling at his cigarette. He might have been sorry to lose his five thousand pounds, but at least he was a free agent who could discard a case when he had had enough of it. Boris was not allowed the luxury of failure. He must either find the woman or prove conclusively that she was dead.

Tomorrow he would start work, and his first visit would be to the detective's office, because there was something in the wording of the last report which didn't ring quite true. Had Paulson's final clue paid off, perhaps? Did he know where the woman was? Could he have located Miss Reilly and intended to let Grant fret for a while and then offer to reveal her whereabouts for a larger fee?

Hardly likely, but the office was his obvious port of call in the morning: tonight he intended to get drunk. Boris helped himself to more vodka and frowned as the telephone rang.

'Orel here.' The instrument felt cold in his grasp. 'Oh, it's you, George. Yes, I saw your father, but I'm afraid I can't tell you what it's all about. As Mr Byrne said, it was a personal matter and I promised not to discuss it with anybody.'

'That does not apply to me, Boris.' George Grant was unusually brusque. 'I have just left my father and he has put me in the picture. For some time he has been trying to contact a woman named Patricia Reilly whom he knew when he was young. A professional inquiry agent failed, but he now appears to think you are some kind of miracle worker who can locate her for him. I am ringing to tell you to do no such thing.'

'I am afraid I have already agreed.' Boris's resentment was directed against George as well as Sir Ernest. Both father and adopted son appeared to think he was under their orders. 'Why should you object to his finding the woman?'

'Because my father is a sick man. He may not have loved his wife, but her death shook him up considerably and probably caused his stroke. Now he is lonely and has developed a fixation about Miss Reilly. He not only wants to meet her again, he intends to marry her, if she will have him.'

'And very naturally you want to prevent that, George.'

'Yes, I damn well do, but not for financial reasons as you appear to imagine.' George had obviously read his thoughts. 'I might be cut out of the will should the marriage take place, but there's little chance of that happening. If the reply to his advertisement was genuine she still hates his guts. What concerns me is my father's mental health and Miss Reilly's safety.' There was a pause and a click on the line as if George had put down a glass.

'Look, Boris, you've talked to the old man yourself, he's told you the whole wretched story, and you must realize how disturbed he is. He believes that his future happiness, his actual salvation depends on finding that woman and gaining her forgiveness and love. It's a complete obsession with him, so what would happen if you did locate her and she rejected him again? He's not a man to accept refusal at the best of times and since the stroke he's not really in control of himself.'

'You're worried that Sir Ernest might go right round the bend, George? We know that he had violent tendencies towards Miss Reilly. He beat her up when she threatened to prevent his engagement, and you think that could happen a second time?'

'There has been a second time; didn't he tell you that?' Boris heard another click of a glass and he wondered if George was also trying to drown his worries in drink. 'After that scene in the restaurant when she threw a cup of coffee at him, he tried to strangle her and the waiters had to pull them apart.

'He's old now, of course, and probably would not make an actual physical attack on Miss Reilly, but I think he might do her immense harm if she showed that her feelings could not be changed. He'd try to ruin her financially for a start, and break up her marriage if she has one. He's a rich and influential man with power to hurt people.'

'I am aware of that.' The vodka and the whisky he had had earlier were fuddling Boris's brain. For an instant he considered telling George that he was not a free agent, but at once rejected it. George seemed to think of him as a friend, but he couldn't trust anybody. Besides, he was beginning to lose his temper.

'George, your concern for Miss Reilly's welfare does you credit, but I've got my own welfare to consider. I am an émigré trying to build a future in this country and, as you say, your father is a powerful man. He is also my employer and he has ordered me to find the woman. If she is alive I intend to do just that, and what happens afterwards is not my concern. And now I am going to ring off, because there is no point in discussing the matter any further.'

He banged down the receiver and stood hunched over it. Outside a clock was striking the hour and the radio music had been replaced by the news.

There had been a mine disaster in France, Hurricane Isabel was still sweeping across Florida, the London dock strike had entered its second week . . . 'In the House of Commons today a committee was set up to inquire into the security arrangements of Her Majesty's prisons. Its seven members are to consist of . . .'

A list of names was read out, but Boris hardly heard them. He was too tired, too bitter and miserable, too sodden with alcohol to hear anything clearly except the voices in his head. His own voice coming in gasps and the voice of Sir Ernest Grant full of self-assurance. 'The information regarding you is lodged in my bank with orders to make it public knowledge if I should die violently.'

Boris turned back to the table and scowled at the photograph on the company report and all at once another face suddenly appeared before Grant's. The heavy, dull-eyed face of the escaped strangler. Harry Alban, psychopath, triple murderer, a human being who should never have been born.

Never been born! Boris had become devoted to English lyric poetry and the phrase brought a passage from 'A Shropshire Lad' to his mind.

> Oh soon, and better so than later
> After long disgrace and scorn,
> You shot dead the household traitor,
> The soul that should not have been born.

Fair enough, he thought. Alban was indeed a man who should never have been conceived, but what about himself? He was a traitor, too, and not only to his country. 'Don't touch me,' Shura had pleaded. 'Please don't touch me, Boris. Don't make me as dirty as yourself.' He also had disgrace and scorn to live with, and in one respect he and the Hangman had much in common. They were both men who had incurred terrible debts and tried to escape from them.

Mrs Nancy Forester had never met Sir Ernest Grant in person, but she shared Boris's hatred of him and it had come welling up while she and the rest of the night shift filed out of the factory. Bloody swine, she said to herself, tightening her threadbare coat and opening her umbrella against the rain that had started to fall. What a life for a woman of her age; working away at a lathe five nights a week to keep Deadly Earnest rich, while Fred had to rot at home and eat his heart out on national benefit.

'So long, Mary. 'Bye, Doreen. See you, Else.' She parted from

her companions outside the gate and hurried away down the long
street running beside the docks: a small, shabbily dressed woman
of fifty-two with a lined face and a chip like a sack of cement on
her thin shoulders. It was ten years since Fred had had his accident;
she had accepted the fact that it was his own fault, but her resentment against Grant would never die.

For, though Fred had lost his hand by disobeying regulations,
he had worked at the plant since he was an apprentice and they
could have paid him compensation. The floor supervisor thought
he'd get it and Mr Sims, the factory manager, had agreed. Then old
Grant had come on the scene and they had changed their minds.

'I am sorry, my dear,' Mr Sims had said and she knew that he
meant it. 'I had hoped that your husband would receive either a
pension or a lump sum to enable you to open a business, but the
decision is not mine to make. Your husband was injured because
the guard of his machine was down and Sir Ernest Grant feels that
compensation is out of the question.'

Mean pig. Mrs Forester shook her head as she turned a corner.
The factory workers had dispersed, and apart from a paper boy
on his rounds and a man slouching along the opposite pavement,
the street was deserted. The solicitor had said that Aly were quite
clearly within their legal right, but they would never have missed
a few hundred pounds; just enough to start her and Fred off in a
business of their own.

Only six, indeed! As usual the clock of St Peter's was slow and
its heavy notes boomed through the morning rain as she crossed
the road. She always took the short cut on her way home from
work, but never at night. After the pubs and coffee bars shut the
churchyard swarmed with teenage hooligans and wasn't safe for
ordinary folk. A coffee bar or a fish shop was the kind of thing
she and Fred had hoped to open with the promised compensation,
and it would have been a decent well-run place, too: catering for
respectable clients, not like most of them these days.

What was the use of thinking about that though? Ernest Grant
had vetoed any compensation, Fred was a cripple rotting on State
aid and she would have to slave away for Aly till she was worn out
and useless. Horrible, mean Ernest Grant.

Mrs Forester walked quickly on along the path between the graves; modern slabs of granite and marble, and flamboyant Victorian pillars and urns and mourning angels. The sound of the rain was increasing and she never heard the footsteps hurrying behind her. She was still thinking of her grievances when the strip of cloth encircled her neck.

Chapter Four

'Danalliance Foundries' – 'The Daneville Pressed Steel Company' – 'The River Dan Quay'. Boris sat gloomily in the bus that was taking him to Paulson's office and watched his employer's citadels slide past. Daneville had a bad parking problem; he rarely took his car into the centre of the town and because of the rain every taxi seemed to have been commandeered. The top deck of the bus was thick with tobacco smoke and steaming raincoats.

'Daneville United F.C.' That was another subsidiary of Allied Concessions. Aly had swallowed a dozen firms in its time but never fully digested them because the policy was to divide and rule and each had retained its own board of directors answerable only to the holding company which meant Sir Ernest Grant. When the old man died, or became senile – he would never retire unless forced to – it would take a strong leader to hold the pack together. Certainly someone much stronger than George.

Was there any foundation for George's anxieties? Boris considered as he wiped condensation from the window and saw the tower of the Allied Building loom before him. It was certain that Sir Ernest had had a bad stroke and strange that such a man should have mellowed enough to pine for his former mistress and feel deep guilt at the way he had treated her. Also, Grant had told him that he himself believed that the reply to his advertisement had been written by Miss Reilly. Everything did seem to suggest mental illness. Megalomania which made him convinced he would win back a woman who only wanted to avoid him.

So what would happen if he failed to win her back? Was George right in thinking that rejection could destroy his sanity completely?

That once again he might attack and injure his lost love as he had done in the past?

Love . . . lost love. Boris closed his eyes briefly and he thought of the way Shura had looked at him when he told her what he was and what he had done. The sudden fear and hostility and revulsion in her face fading to resignation when she understood that her feelings were unimportant because they had no escape from each other; two unfriendly prisoners doomed to share their solitary confinement.

And George's worries were unimportant too. Sane or insane, Ernest Grant had to be obeyed and if she existed, Miss Reilly must be found. He was just a puppet dancing at the end of a string and would probably remain one till Sir Ernest's dying day.

It was pleasant to think of Grant dying. A long, agonizing illness, a motor accident like his wife's; perhaps murder. The old man must have made a legion of enemies in his time and Boris was quite certain he was not the only dancer in the puppet show.

Or if the bastard could meet up with this joker one dark night. He picked up a newspaper some former passenger had left on the seat. The prison inquiry had kept Harry Alban's escape to the fore and his life history was outlined in the centre pages. Orphanage boy . . . started work as a builder's labourer when he was fifteen and remained with the same firm in East London till his arrest nine years ago . . . His employers had stated that he was very strong and a willing worker, though slow-witted in the extreme and in need of constant supervision . . . No motive had been discovered for his murders and he had been found 'unfit to plead' . . . The victims were all women in their mid-forties whom he did not know and each had been strangled with a necktie. There had been no robbery or sexual assault on them. A fourth victim would have been claimed, but she had managed to scream and after a hard struggle Alban was overpowered by a group of men who were leaving a public house.

A very strong fellow, indeed. Boris had an image of Sir Ernest's face contorting; there was a tie around his neck and the Hangman's hands were tugging it tighter. An attractive notion, but quite unobtainable. Harry Alban's mania was directed only against middle-aged women, and in any case Grant's death by violence was a possibility to be dreaded.

'Let me repeat my earlier warnings, Orel,' the old man had said towards the end of the interview. 'Forget any stupid ambitions about killing me. With that statement lodged at the bank, it is in your interests that I remain in good health.'

'Inkerman Road.' The conductor called out the stop and Boris pushed aside the paper and negotiated the lurching stairs to the platform. The rain was still falling heavily, and as he tightened his trench coat he felt a bulge in the pocket. Sir Ernest had described Paulson's safe to him and with the stethoscope he had purchased on his way to the bus, the combination should present few problems.

But would the safe contain anything to help him, he wondered while he hurried through the rain. Was he right in thinking that Paulson might have had a clue to Miss Reilly's whereabouts and intended to let Grant sweat for a while and then offer to reveal her for a higher fee? Boris had sensed a hint of that in the detective's last report to Grant, but probably he was being too hopeful and over-suspicious. It was almost certain that Paulson had found the case too difficult, as he stated, and accepted another which necessitated his closing the office for a time.

Balaclava Square. All the street signs commemorated the last open conflict between England and Russia and Boris grinned at the irony. Lord Cardigan House: like the rest of the area the block must have been put up shortly after the Crimean War and it was an imposing pile of Victorian Gothic with a turreted porch over the doorway and decorative towers and pinnacles sprouting from the roof. But the once mellow facings of red sandstone were dark with grime and pockmarked by weather and the building was obviously coming to the end of its life. To the left lay a stretch of recently cleared land, and beyond that demolition workers were tearing into its next-but-one neighbour.

'Gresham & Brown, Solicitors and Commissioners for Oaths.' 'Jack Baxter, Turf Accountant.' There was a porter behind the reception desk, but he looked almost as old as the building and was completely absorbed in a sporting paper. Boris ignored him and studied the tenant index boards which were set in Oxford frames and resembled rolls of honour.

'The Northmoorland Inquiry Agency.' The aged porter glanced indifferently at him as he crossed over to the lift, and then returned to his deliberations on the chances of Daneville United and Castle Landon drawing with Chelsea and Stoke City next Saturday.

Here I go again, Boris thought while the archaic machine creaked up towards the top floor. Yesterday a respectable businessman, now a felon. And one day, if I fail . . . a stiff.

But he wasn't going to fail. There was too much at stake for that. Last night in his drunken misery he had considered suicide, but now the thought had left him. He would find Miss Reilly or prove that she was dead and rely on Ernest Grant to keep his promise of silence. An arrow showed him that Paulson's office was at the end of a long corridor and the only person he passed was another very old man resembling a Dickensian clerk who was shambling along with a deed box clutched against his black coat and striped trousers.

'Number 450, The Northmoorland Private Inquiry Agency. Proprietor, Ex-Detective Inspector Eric Paulson, C.I.D.' The door had a frosted glass panel and a spring lock and it trembled as a series of thuds joined the rattle of the drills. The demolition crew were battering down the condemned building with a crane and a metal ball.

'Yes, here I come, Inspector Paulson. And though you said that you couldn't locate the blasted woman, let's hope that you filed a bit of information about her.' Boris leaned against the door and slipped a strip of mica into the gap he had created. The mica eased back the tongue of the lock and he stepped into the office and closed the door behind him.

The reception room had not been used or cleaned for several days. A window was partly open and dust from the demolition works had drifted in and lay on the parquet floor, the periodicals on the table and on the top of a filing cabinet. A vase of dead autumn roses stood on the window ledge and at either side of the window a collection of framed photographs, certificates and press cuttings were displayed.

In his notes Ernest Grant had suggested that the detective might have had to go abroad because he was mixed up in some unsavoury business which made England unhealthy for him. But judging from the photographs there was nothing unsavoury about Eric Paulson.

Some of the photographs showed the inspector in plain clothes, in others he wore uniform, but his expression did not vary. In each pose he radiated calm authority. A firm chin tilted forward towards the camera, a big nose jutting out above the neatly trimmed moustache and eyes that glowed with self-assurance and honesty. Poses designed to show that he was a man who would lay down his life for a client providing the business was entirely above board. Boris could imagine him stating his terms. 'I take no cases outside the law, sir. Nothing that my friends and late colleagues of the force would object to.'

No. Paulson did not appear to be the type of person who would run from the threats of criminals, but he was obviously a man with a high opinion of himself. Boris glanced at the other exhibits. Certificates for bravery and competence and records of former cases, 'MYSTERY MURDER CRACKED . . . Personal Triumph for Inspector Eric Paulson.' The collection might be intended to impress visitors, but he suspected that their owner's vanity came first.

'Good for you, Eric old boy.' Boris walked towards a door marked STRICTLY PRIVATE which must lead to the detective's inner sanctum. It was already ajar and started to swing open as the metal ball did its work and the floor shuddered before a crash of falling brickwork. As if encouraging him to enter the door moved farther and farther back, but Boris stopped in his tracks.

Facing him was a huge, old-fashioned safe with two more photographs of Paulson displayed above it. One showed him as proud and full of authority as before, but in the other he had a friendly smile to show the more human side of his nature. In both of them his eyes appeared to be looking down at the woman who was crouched beside the safe.

Her head was in shadow and her back towards him, but though Boris could not tell whether she was young or old it was quite clear what she was doing. Her right hand was on the dial of the lock and in her left a notebook. She consulted the book, turned the dial twice and pulled open the door.

Though he had moved quietly, she had heard him. Silence had followed the crash of brickwork and she straightened and swung round very quickly. A young woman who might have been beautiful if her eyes were not so full of terror and her mouth wide open as she prepared to scream. But no scream came. For a full ten seconds she stood swaying silently in front of him and then staggered towards him and Boris understood.

It was not he, but the contents of the safe, that had frightened her. The swollen, hideous thing that squatted in the metal box like the victim of a medieval 'little ease'. Its features were no longer calm and commanding, no gleam of honesty showed in the eyes and the lips did not smile, because there was nothing for them to smile about. If Eric Paulson had left Daneville he had come back to die. Judging by the signs of rigor he had been dead for some time.

*

'Mr Paulson gave you the safe combination on the day you left for France.' The next-door office happened to be vacant, but still furnished and Inspector Peter Palmer lounged behind the desk of its former tenant.

'He said there was a chance he might be out of town himself when you got back, Mrs Renton, and if so, you were to collect the salary and expenses due to you.' Palmer eyed the woman seated beside Boris and made another note in his shorthand pad. The body had been removed now, but beyond the party wall his assistants were still at work checking for fingerprints, taking photographs and listing the dead man's belongings.

'Ruth Renton,' Palmer had written earlier. 'Aged twenty-eight – widow – native of Daneville – Eric's part-time assistant and secretary for eleven months.' His final entry read 'In the clear', and he picked up the passport lying open before him and handed it back to her. The doctor had been reasonably certain that Paulson had been dead for between a week and ten days and the passport proved that

Mrs Renton had been abroad during that period and returned to England only last night.

'Wasn't it somewhat unusual for the office to be left unattended for days on end, madam?'

'Not especially, Inspector. Mr Paulson had an arrangement with David Gresham of the Viking Agency. If we were both away all our business was transferred to them.' Ruth Renton spoke slowly and haltingly as though she were using an unfamiliar language. It was an hour and a half since she had opened the safe but she still felt dazed with shock. 'We used to put a notice on the door referring callers to the Viking people.'

'Which was not left in position this time, nor were there any instructions to forward the mail. There's quite a pile at the reception desk, but I'm pretty certain it won't help us. Few murderers are obliging enough to put their intentions in writing; worse luck.' Palmer grimaced over his notes. 'Did Mr Paulson go into details about this business which might take him away from Daneville?'

'No, Inspector, and it may not have been a business trip. I had the impression that he felt in need of a holiday, but I can't really be sure. I was too busy thinking about my own assignment to remember what he actually said to me when I left for France.'

Ruth's quarry had been a clergyman; an Anglican canon noted for extreme piety whose mental health had been causing his flock some distress. On several occasions he had informed his church-wardens that he was a reincarnation of John the Baptist and the time was approaching for him to leave the wilderness. After he failed to return from his annual pilgrimage to Lourdes, they feared that overwork had produced a loss of memory and enlisted Paulson's help. When Ruth ran him to earth she had discovered that the allusions to the Baptist were jocular. The good canon had no intention of returning to the wilderness of Daneville and was comfortably installed at Cannes with one of his wealthier parishioners: the widow of a betting-shop proprietor.

'Your preoccupation was perfectly natural, madam.' The inspector's smile was gallant and he underlined the entry 'In the clear'. He was glad to do that because Mrs Renton was an attractive piece and he wouldn't have liked to think of her killing Eric; certainly not in that way. Palmer had been Paulson's subordinate for two years before he left the force and they had thoroughly disliked each other, but there was no denying that it was a nasty way to die, and somebody Eric had trusted must be his murderer. That was all they could be sure of at the moment. There were no bruises to imply a struggle, no suggestion that he had been doped, so he had been taken by surprise. A man or woman had walked over to him while he stood on the threshold of the safe and slammed the door home with him behind it. Cause of death, suffocation, and it would have taken the poor bleeder a long time to lose consciousness.

Had Eric been having it off with this lass, he wondered? Probably not, because he was a cold fish and completely in love with himself. Now, if he had been her boss . . . Inspector Palmer fought to conceal his admiration. Mrs Renton was a real smasher, though naturally she wasn't looking her best at the moment. Dark hair and eyes contrasting excitingly with a fair skin, and a mouth that hinted at sensuality. Full breasts and wide, child-bearing hips, too. The inspector fancied women with a bit of meat on 'em. Unlike his late colleague he was not clear-eyed, firm-featured and dedicated to his work. He was an idle, easy-going man with the tanned complexion of the habitual beer drinker and three maxims which he followed to the letter. 'Play a waiting game.' 'Never run when you can walk, or walk when you can ride.' 'Allow the blighter enough rope and he'll hang himself.' But in spite of that, there was a shrewd brain inside his balding skull and Daneville's criminal elements knew that there weren't many flies on old 'Pussy' Palmer.

No, the lovely Ruth Renton had not killed Eric or been an accomplice to his murder. Half a dozen witnesses were certain that her shock was quite genuine and he could write off this Russian fellow as well. It was a bit of a coincidence that she and Orel had discovered the body together and at first he had considered that they might have been accomplices in some way. That was why he had decided to hold a joint interview and watch how the one reacted to the other's answers.

Now he knew he was wrong, though friend Orel was a dark

horse, to say the least. A Soviet defector who had landed a job with Aly, and was important enough to deal with Sir Ernest Grant personally. The inspector tore his eyes from Ruth's shapely bosom and frowned at Boris.

Orel's story was that Grant had decided to employ an inquiry agent for some confidential business and sent him to call on Eric Paulson unannounced and see if he appeared efficient and reliable. Orel had refused to state what the business was without Sir Ernest's permission, but Palmer could make a guess. There had been an outbreak of pilfering at the docks recently and Aly feared that police intervention would cause trouble with the unions. A private detective might have seemed a natural compromise.

But obviously old Grant and his minions had not killed Eric and he wouldn't press the matter. It didn't do to annoy Deadly Earnest; not in Daneville – not if you hoped to retire on a super's pension. He was about to dismiss Boris when his sergeant came into the room.

'We've finished the inventories of the safe and filing cabinet, sir.' He laid a folder before him. 'To my mind there's something a bit odd about the more recent case listings.'

'Right, Sergeant.' Palmer dismissed him and opened the folder. 'There's no need for me to detain you any longer, Mr Orel.'

'Thank you, Inspector. But if you don't object I'd rather like to stay.' Boris looked protectively towards Ruth. If Palmer agreed he was bound to hear something about Paulson's file on the Reilly woman. 'As Mrs Renton's had such a shock I think I should see her home, if she'd let me.'

'A policewoman could do that, but I've no objection to your staying.' The inspector's piggy eyes twinkled. The Russian was on the make and he didn't blame him. If he'd been in a position to do so, he'd have tried the same thing himself.

'Umhm. There were six hundred and thirty-three pounds in the safe, so we can rule out robbery as a motive.' He bent over the inventory. 'Did Eric Paulson usually keep such a large cash sum on hand, Mrs Renton?'

'Almost always. Most people with information to sell demand cash payments: hotel servants, taxi drivers, booking clerks and so on.' She had been engaged in a sordid business, Ruth thought. Divorce evidence had formed the bulk of it, but there were also employers who suspected their tills were being dipped into, parents anxious to know more about a son's or daughter's intended spouse, missing persons like her clergyman basking on the Riviera with his widow.

A sordid, but not really a dangerous business, because Eric Paulson never involved himself with anything he considered to be an affair for the police. Once a woman with a teenage son on heroin had asked him to find the pusher and he had coldly referred her to the C.I.D. As she had told Palmer earlier on, Ruth could think of many people who might resent Eric's activities, but not a single one likely to have killed him.

Somebody had killed him, though. Somebody posing as a friend or a client or an informant had lured him into that huge, half-empty safe which he had bought to establish a status, and slammed the door home.

Poor Eric. Though he had been a good enough employer, he was too conceited and full of himself to inspire affection, but his must have been an agonizing death, and she racked her brains for a possible suspect.

Nothing came however. Her mind felt dull and numb as though she hadn't slept for days, and all she could think about was that heavy door swinging open and the glazed eyes of her employer staring at her from the bloated face. Then she had swung round trying to scream and seen the man standing in the doorway. Oblivious of everything except fear and horror she had staggered towards him for protection, and the scream had come at the instant he caught her in his arms. A constant, high-pitched sound that she hardly recognized as her own and it had continued till doors banged, feet came hurrying along the corridor and the room was suddenly full of people.

'Ah, this is what Sergeant Martin considered odd.' The inspector frowned at a page. A moment ago he had been thinking about his lunch, but now he was interested. 'All your cases are filed up to the end of September, but there is nothing listed since then. Six weeks without an assignment. That appears a bit unlikely, Mrs Renton.'

'It's just not true.' Ruth frowned back at him. 'We took on four cases during the period. Canon Gievson, whom I've told you about. Major Blacker; that was divorce business. I can't recall his address, but you'll find it in the local directory. Miss Reilly.' Though the inspector did not notice it, she broke off abruptly at the name and hurried on to the next. 'Mr Maxwell, the headmaster of Lowther Road School. There had been some vandalism in the building and he wanted to find the culprits without involving you.'

'Bloody fool.' Palmer recorded the list with a scowl. The sight of a few uniforms usually puts paid to that kind of monkey business.

'So probably the killer removed his own file and the others as well to fox us. What about the third case you mentioned: this Miss Reilly? What was her trouble?'

'I can't remember much about it, Inspector. Eric only mentioned the case to me in passing.' If Palmer had been watching Ruth's face he would have seen a flush. 'As far as I can recall, Miss Reilly was a middle-aged woman who had recently become engaged. Her fiancé was persuading her to draw out her life savings and invest it in a business and she was worried that he might be conning her.'

'And if the bastard was and Eric had rumbled him, he could be the horse for my money. Swindlers don't usually resort to violence, but when they do, they make a meal of it.' Palmer considered the careers of the infamous Haig and Hume and 'Brides in the Bath' Smith and his own namesake, William Palmer; 'Saintly Doctor Billy,' the Rugely poisoner.

'Miss Reilly's address, Mrs Renton? Did she live locally?' He sighed as Ruth shook her head. 'The woman may be in great danger, you know.'

'I'm sorry, Inspector, but I can't even remember her first name. And could I go now? I still feel a bit faint.'

'Of course.' Palmer stood up. 'But do keep thinking about this woman, Mrs Renton. As I said, she could be in danger and any detail that occurs to you might help. Goodbye for the present and we'll remain in touch with you both.' He led them out to the corridor and turned into Paulson's office.

'Sergeant Martin, I want a general call put out for a Miss Reilly.

No first name known, but she's middle-aged, probably lower middle-class and must have been domiciled in this area recently. She was contemplating marriage, so check the registry offices and the churches; also the banks, post offices and building societies. She'd saved some money and may be the victim of a con man.'

A nasty death, he thought, looking at the safe while the sergeant telephoned his orders. Darkness, foul air, no sound except your limbs beating against the metal and your lungs fighting for oxygen. What a way to die.

I hated your guts, Eric, but you were a copper once so you'll have preferential treatment. We always get cop killers and we'll find the bastard who 'coffined you up', as the undertakers say.

'No, don't ring off yet, Sergeant.' The inspector's empty belly was troubling him and he consulted his watch. 'Get through to the canteen and have 'em send some lunch over. I saw there was roast with two veg and Yorkshire on the menu today.' His eyes gleamed at the prospect. 'So tell the lying sods not to fob us off with anything else, eh?'

Chapter Five

'Feeling any better?' Boris brought over a second round of drinks and sat down facing Ruth. It was lunch time, the saloon bar was crowded and they had been lucky to find a table to themselves. Outside it was still raining, and as on the bus, the atmosphere of the room was thick with smoke and condensation.

'Just a bit.' Ruth smiled at him as she raised the glass, but she was still numbed by her experience. The brandy was helping her, she was grateful to Boris for taking her to the pub, but he worked for Grant and she was trying to keep on her guard. 'I just can't really take in that Eric's dead, Mr Orel. He was a strong man and he held a black belt for judo. To be pushed into that safe shows he trusted his killer completely.'

'Unless the killer appeared to be no physical match for him; a woman perhaps.' Boris held out his cigarettes and lit one for her. 'If Miss Reilly's fiancé was conning her, Paulson would hardly have trusted him and the inspector's theory is wrong.' Though he spoke very gently there was a touch of cynicism in Boris's manner. 'Were you fond of Paulson, Mrs Renton?'

'Not fond, but I'll always feel grateful to Eric. I used to be my husband's secretary and when he was killed I wanted a job that would take me out of myself, as they say. Eric took me on because he considered that I had a prying mind. Not much of a compliment, but it was exactly the kind of work I needed.' Ruth considered her husband as Boris asked a second question. Poor Allan, who imagined himself to be a shrewd businessman when he was only a gambler and incapable of forming a balanced judgment or accepting advice. It was no wonder that his ventures collapsed one after the other.

'My husband was drowned, Mr Orel. He operated a hovercraft service to Ireland with two old, unreliable machines and one of them foundered. The crew and all the passengers were rescued but Allan died. I think he killed himself.' A siren joined the drone of the traffic and Ruth imagined the rescue ships approaching the survivors and Allan swimming away from them. The hovercraft's reliability certificate had been forged and failure would have been coupled with criminal proceedings if he had lived.

Yes, Allan Renton had been a sad man, and so was this Boris Orel. Ruth studied him through the smoke, remembering how she had stumbled from the hideous thing in the safe and he had caught her in his arms and kept repeating. 'All right, my dear . . . it's all right, I say . . . all right, all right, all right.'

Very kind, very gentle, very appealing, but sadness surrounded him like a physical presence, as was to be expected. He had told Palmer that he was a Russian defector and he must have given up his friends and perhaps a family. Now, like herself, he was quite alone. 'Do you think they'll ever get Eric's killer, Mr Orel?'

'I know they'll do their darnedest to find him – or her. He was an ex-policeman, remember.' Almost imperceptibly Boris's manner was altering. He still sounded sympathetic, but the cynicism had increased. 'But I know something else, Mrs Renton. If people go on lying to the police, the killer will go free.'

'What do you mean?' Ruth's hand clenched tightly around her glass. 'Just what are you implying?'

'You know perfectly well what I mean. For some reason you don't want the police to know about Ernest Grant's interest in Miss Reilly, and you let her name slip out by accident. You then deceived the inspector with a . . .' he paused in search of the collo-quial phrase, 'a cock-and-bull story about an engagement and some man persuading her to part with her savings. So can we have the truth now, my dear? You may have deceived Inspector Palmer, but you can't deceive me. I work for Grant and I know about the real Miss Reilly.'

'I was a fool, wasn't I?' Ruth was staring down at the table and through the window behind her. Boris heard more sirens and saw an ambulance and a police car weaving through the traffic. 'I should have known I couldn't get away with it, but I was too dazed to concentrate and I didn't think I would do any harm. Sir Ernest had sworn Eric to secrecy and I felt I should respect his promise. Quite obviously the Reilly case has nothing to do with Eric's murder, and after I slipped up and mentioned her name I had to invent some kind of story.'

'I am sure that Sir Ernest will appreciate your loyalty.' Boris inclined his head in a mocking bow. Ruth Renton must be right in believing that the quest for Paddy Reilly had nothing to do with the detective's death. Most probably the killer was mentioned in some document written by Paulson after she left for France, and he had removed it and all the more recent files to create confusion. But her story about a con man had certainly increased that confu-sion, and misleading the police was a serious matter.

'But loyalty is not your only motive, is it?' Boris took a swig of beer. 'It is the reward that interests you. You hope to earn the five thousand pounds that Grant promised to pay Paulson.'

'And why shouldn't I?' Ruth looked him straight in the face. 'There is nothing wrong in helping an old, lonely man to find a woman he loves. We both know that Sir Ernest can't have anything to do with Eric's murder. He'd hardly have sent you to the office if that was the case.' She stubbed out her cigarette and flushed angrily. 'Well, what are you waiting for, Mr Orel? Finish your drink and go round to the police station like a good citizen and tell them that I lied.'

'Not just yet, Ruth.' Boris's smile was friendly again and his cynicism was directed against himself. 'Sir Ernest's wishes are my law and he considers that the less the police and the newspapers know about his quest the better. Your lack of ethics is to my advantage, so we had better become allies. But what you don't know is that Paulson intended to drop the case while you were away. He stated that it was too difficult for him which means it will be just as difficult for us.' He drained the rest of his beer and stood up.

'Now, I'm going to get another round of drinks and after we've had them we'll go round to my office and start to pool our resources, and . . .'

Like everyone else in the room Boris fell silent. The door had banged open and five policemen burst into the room. They had their truncheons drawn and one of them held an Alsatian straining on a short leather strap.

'Please stay exactly where you are, ladies and gentlemen.' A sergeant raised his voice. 'There is no cause for alarm, but please don't move.' He nodded to the men behind him and they spread out and started to pace purposefully forward, eyeing the male customers as they did so. Boris noticed that they merely glanced at most of the men present, but those who were broad-shouldered and heavily built were given hard, scrutinizing stares.

'What the hell's all this about, Sergeant?' The landlord had ignored the orders and hurried across to him. 'I keep a decent house here. You can't come barging in here with riot sticks and a bloody dog.'

'Keep quiet, Mr Phelps. You don't want people to panic any more than we do.' The policeman lowered his face and whispered savagely, but Boris and Ruth were close enough to hear most of what he said.

'. . . woman's body . . . found in churchyard . . . strangled . . . fellow looking like the bastard who did it seen coming in here . . . course we know who it was . . . that crazy Hangman.'

'This was taken during the last journey of the season, Miss Robbins.' George Grant switched on his pocket tape recorder and the tiny plastic spools started to revolve. With them came a hiss of

escaping steam, a jolt of wood and metal, and the rumble of other
wheels – the heavy, cast-iron wheels of tank locomotive Number
3, *Owen Tudor* pulling out of Port Olwyn station. George closed
his eyes and imagined the journey. The little engine building up
pressure along the causeway beside the sea as its blower increased
the draught and the whistle hooted on the sharp curve before the
level crossing. He could smell the blazing fire and the hot oil and
metal as he listened, feel the lurch of the platform beneath his feet
as they rounded the bend, and see the hills around him gay with
heather and bracken and here and there patches of rhododendrons
like clouds of purple smoke.

'Listen to the engine beats increasing, Miss Robbins.' In his
mind's eye, George watched the gauges, felt the regulator handle
warm in his grasp and glanced at his fireman busily at work.
Complete and utter happiness.

'Damnation.' There was a sudden click and the tape recorder
became silent. 'The wretched thing keeps doing that. There's a
faulty switch that I've been meaning to have repaired for weeks.
Once or twice it's even started to record off its own bat which
could lead to an embarrassing situation some day.' He pushed the
machine aside with a grin and produced a stack of photographs
from his drawer.

'Some of these might interest you. This is an interior of one
of the first-class buffet cars. She's all ready for service when we
reopen in the spring.'

'It's very grand indeed, sir.' His secretary studied the print, seeing a profusion of brass and mahogany, armchairs deeply uphol-
stered with horsehair, a royal-blue carpet and the company's crest
of a raven and a dove emblazoned on the panels.

'Did you rebuild it completely?' Miss Robbins tried to simulate
enthusiasm. She was very fond of George, but how she wished
that he did not expect her to share his passion for boiler capacities
and piston speeds and patent couplings. Still, the buffet car was a
bit nearer to her taste.

'More or less. Right up from the chassis, in fact. The coach had
been parked in an open siding for years and all the timbers were
rotted. Here is one taken before we started work.'

'You must spend a terrible lot of money.' Ethel Robbins frowned. George was moderately well off, she supposed, but she sensed that he had been worried recently. He was always slightly indrawn except when discussing his hobby, but much more so of late. At times she had found him staring at some quite routine business reports as though he could not make head nor tail of them. He was also drinking a great deal as well. 'When should the railway start to show a profit, sir?'

'God alone knows – probably never.' George shook his head over a third snapshot: the tiny terminus at Bryncir and the station master's quarters he had converted for his own use. The venture had given him so much pleasure, but money was still running through their fingers. Already one of his partners had opted out and, if more followed suit, the old railway might come to a stand-still again. The rolling stock left to rot, the buildings to decay while grass and willow herb flourished over the tracks.

'Apart from running expenses there is still so much actual rebuilding to be done. This viaduct, for instance, will have to be strengthened before next season and some of the arches are over fifty feet high. There are two main factors against us. We're a standard-gauge line and tourists don't regard us as amusing and quaint, as they do the Ffestiniog Railway. Also the area is so depressed and underpopulated. The line was built to serve the slate quarries at Bryncir, but after the industry collapsed the place became a virtual ghost town with only the scenery to attract visitors. Still, people may start to take notice of us one day and our luck change.'

'I do hope so.' Miss Robbins looked pointedly at her watch, thinking of her cosy flat with the chain and the Chubb lock on the door. The evening paper had shown that her fears were justified, and she'd try to get a taxi home tonight.

'But if you have no more letters for me, could I get off home, sir? We know that that madman is here in Daneville and he's killed again. I won't feel safe till I've got my door locked behind me – no single woman will.'

'Yes, you go along, Miss Robbins, but do try and be reasonable.' George had also read the paper. When Mrs Forester failed to return home her husband had informed the police and the body had been discovered later by some children playing in the churchyard. She was of the same physical type as Alban's former victims, though slightly older than them, she had been strangled with a necktie, and there had been no robbery or sexual assault. Without committing themselves, a police spokesman and the *Daneville Star* made it quite clear that the Hangman was the only possible suspect.

'It's less than five hours since they discovered the body, so how can they presuppose that that "madman", as you call him, is responsible? The senior psychiatrist at Seamont was certain that Harry Alban was no longer dangerous, and I believe that to be true. I've visited Seamont, Miss Robbins, and I've sat in Harry's cell and talked to him. Fundamentally the poor chap's become a gentle creature.' George lit a cigarette and shook his head. 'But just because he's on the run, you and everyone else convict him out of hand.'

'I think it's obvious he did it, sir.' Ethel Robbins might like George, but his humanitarian feelings towards criminals infuriated her. In her opinion, homicidal maniacs should be shot out of hand like the wild animals they were. 'Seamont is not far away from here. Surely it's too much of a coincidence for another insane strangler to be operating in the same area.'

'You witch-hunters always stress the word "insane".' George pulled hard at his cigarette and watched the smoke drift away to the ceiling. 'If some quite rational person had a grudge against Mrs Forester, isn't it possible that he might have killed her and used Alban's method to throw suspicion on him?'

'Possible, but hardly likely, I would have thought.' She shrugged and then reached out for the house telephone which had started to ring. 'Oh, good evening, sir. Yes, he's still here and I'll tell him at once, sir.' There was deep respect in her manner as she took the message.

'It was your father. He is in his office and he wants to see you immediately.'

'Thank you, Miss Robbins. You go along now.' George started to gather up the photographs as she wished him good night. 'Lock your door, look under your bed and say a prayer, if it makes you feel better. But I give you my word that the bogeyman won't get you.'

'Come in, George.' Sir Ernest's study at home might be gloomy, but his office was even more so; a functional cell entirely devoted to business. The windows were curtained because he found that daylight distracted him and George often thought of the room as part of some military bunker buried deep under the earth.

'I am going to ask you a question, my boy, and you need not be frightened about answering it. Nothing you tell me will go beyond these walls.' He waved George to a chair beside his desk and stared down at him. 'Did you kill Eric Paulson?'

'Paulson? Did I kill him?' George's head shot back as though the old man had struck him. 'You really must be mad, Father. I didn't even know he was dead.'

'He's dead all right. Paulson was murdered over a week ago and his secretary and your friend, Boris Orel, found the body this morning. Somebody locked him in a safe and let him suffocate.' Grant considered the detective's last moments while he studied George's expression, but unlike Inspector Palmer he did not think of them in physical terms, the lack of light and sound and air, but in terms of loneliness. The terror of a soul that had been buried alive and cut off from its fellows for ever. 'Did you push him into that safe, George?'

'Of course I didn't.' To calm his nerves George fiddled with his empty pipe. 'Be reasonable, Father. What possible motive could I have had?'

'To stop him carrying out my instructions to locate Miss Reilly, and in a way I don't blame you, George. I never gave you the affection you needed and when Madge died you thought we'd have a closer relationship. But after I told you about Paddy, you became desperate to stop me finding her. You thought a third person would come between us and spoil everything.'

'I am desperately worried, Father, but not for that reason. It's over thirty years since you saw the woman and she has made it quite clear that she wants to have nothing to do with you.' George's face was livid above his beard. 'She will never forgive you, so put this obsession out of your mind. Leave Miss Reilly alone for her sake as well as your own. If you do find her I think you might become really ill, Father.'

'I won't, my boy, because Paddy will forgive me. I am going to win back her love and ask her to marry me and there is nothing that you or anybody else can do about it.' Grant took a glass and a bottle of whisky from a cabinet. 'Now, take some Dutch courage, George, and tell me the truth. Did you kill Paulson?'

'No, I did not.' George was almost shouting as he filled the glass. 'I hoped and prayed that he would be unsuccessful and he was. You told me yourself that he was giving up the case, so why should I worry about him?'

'Paulson only said he *might* have to drop the case, and I'm wondering if somebody offered him money to do so.' Grant watched George down the neat whisky. 'But if the money was not enough and he decided to honour his obligations to me . . . If he told you to go to hell, George, and said that he'd find Paddy for me . . .'

'I did not kill Paulson, Father.' George saw that there was a little nervous tic beating beneath the old man's left cheek. 'His murder couldn't have any connection with your business. Private detectives must make scores of enemies and the police will run down the person responsible soon enough. Father, I swear that I had nothing to do with his death.' George reached out and grasped his hand. 'But surely it should be a warning to you. Like myself you are a religious man, so doesn't this show you that you're going against the divine will by looking for the woman? For the love of God forget her.'

'Very well, I accept your word, my boy.' Grant drew away from him and shook his head. 'But you're wrong about the divine will, you know. It is because of that that I am looking for Paddy. When I was ill and half-conscious after the stroke, I heard God's voice clearly. He told me that I am ordained to find Paddy . . . I had to tell her how sorry I was and win her back. I'll do it, too, George. Paulson may be dead, but Orel is my man and he's taken over for me.' Grant had appeared sad and bewildered, but now his confidence had returned. 'Nobody is going to kill my tame Russian because he's very smart indeed and he'll bring Paddy and me together again.

'Yes, help yourself to another drink, my boy. I believe that you had nothing to do with Paulson's death, but I'm going to give you a warning. Don't try to persuade Orel against helping me, because it will get you nowhere. Paddy will be found and when she is you'll realize just how stupid you've been. Excuse me.'

The intercom light was flashing on his desk and he pressed the switch. 'Hullo, Michael, I suppose you're ringing to tell me that our friends have arrived. Good, I'll join them in the conference room shortly, but it won't do any harm to keep them waiting. We've got the whip hand on this deal, so they can cool their heels for a few minutes. By the way, Michael, I suppose you've heard about that woman who was strangled by the escaped maniac this morning. She was one of our operators at the Hangerton Road plant, so we'd better be represented at the funeral. Send a wreath over and have one of the directors attend. Lord Blanchland will do nicely; he not only looks like a deaf mute, but behaves like one. Didn't say a word at the last two board meetings. See you soon, then.'

He switched off the set and frowned at George who had emptied his glass a second time. 'You're drinking a lot these days, aren't you, my boy? Perhaps it's not I but you who are in need of a psychiatrist. Now, what was I saying before Michael rang? Yes, about Orel finding Paddy.' His frown deepened and then he smiled faintly. 'When he does find her, you may be in for a quite a shock, George.'

Chapter Six

Why on earth should Ernest Grant have detailed Boris to locate the woman? They were in Boris's office now and once again Ruth asked herself the question. How could a Russian expatriate whose avowed occupation was market research be expected to do better than a professional detective? Surely the obvious course would have been to employ another inquiry agency?

And why was Boris frightened? She watched him make a fresh entry in his notebook. What hold had old Grant over him? He had appeared to be joking when he said that Grant's wishes were his law, but she sensed that he was telling the exact truth. After they left the pub – the police search had proved fruitless and the man resembling Harry Alban had turned out to be a perfectly inoffensive commercial traveller – she had tried to pump him, but Boris had shrugged her questions brusquely aside and kept returning to the subject of Miss Reilly. Ruth wanted to find the woman for the sake of five thousand pounds, but she was quite sure that his reward was much greater.

'When Grant first approached him, Paulson seemed hesitant to take the case?' Boris glanced up from his notes. 'Why was that, Ruth? Conscience about hounding a woman whose one wish was to remain free of Grant?'

'Certainly not that. Eric had a legal, not a moral conscience, and he would accept any assignment that paid well, providing it was not criminal.' Ruth looked around the office which was rather gay with wall maps and coloured graphs showing Aly's trade with the Soviet Union and its satellite countries. Beside the nearest graph hung an icon of the Virgin.

'Eric was to be paid purely by results and he knew that Grant had had a stroke. For a time he was worried that he might be setting out on a wild-goose chase. Because the woman's name occurs in the song he suspected that the old man might have dreamed up the whole thing and she was just a figment of his imagination.

'It's an Irish ballad that goes something like this, Boris.' He had shaken his head in bewilderment and Ruth quoted, ' "Come back, Paddy Reilly, to Ballyjamesduff. Come back, Paddy Reilly, to me." '

'So, that's what started Grant's search for her. "Come back, Paddy Reilly to me." ' Boris repeated the line. 'He told me that when he was semi-conscious in hospital he heard some song on the radio and kept seeing her face all the time.

'A strange coincidence, though it doesn't help us at all. But at least these notes show that Paulson checked on Grant's story and found that the gist of it was true. Miss Reilly was a real person listed in the official records and so forth.'

'Yes, a friendly agency in London did that for him.' Ruth lit a cigarette and tried to recall what Paulson had told her. The files at Somerset House proved that a girl named Patricia Anderson Reilly had been born at Castle Landon, a town to the north-east of Dane-

ville, on June 8th, 1911. But there were no records to show that she
had married, died, been issued with a passport, or changed her
name by deed poll.

With at least the birth verified Paulson had started work on his
own. Grant had refused his request to enter another advertisement, considering that the woman might be put on her guard and
change her place of residence, and the detective had gone north to
Otterburn, the town where the letter had been posted. Drawing
a blank there he had started his next inquiries at Castle Landon in
the hope of tracing her life story forward from the past.

A series of dead ends came up. Paddy was an only child and
both her parents were killed when the town was bombed in 'forty-
two. After the war the area where they had lived was demolished
to make way for a council estate, and there was not a neighbour or
a shopkeeper left who remembered the family.

The education authorities merely confirmed Grant's statements. Their records showed that Paddy had been an intelligent
child, matriculating at the local grammar school and winning a
scholarship to study zoology at London University. She had left
without a degree during her third year, shortly after she had started
to live with Ernest Grant.

That was that. From the day she and Grant met in the restaurant, the trails ran out and Paddy Reilly had vanished into thin air.

'Zoology? Yes, he mentions that she was fond of animals.' Boris
made another entry. Grant's notes regarding Miss Reilly's character also stated that she had a passion for tidiness. That seemed
to clash with a love of dogs and horses which was so strong that
Grant had considered it unwholesome. She had kept a dog during
the time they lived together and reading between the lines Boris
fancied that Grant had greatly resented the animal.

'And that's all Paulson discovered before you left for France?'

'All that he actually told me, but I felt that he was getting somewhere with the case. He was in a good mood and joked about the
woman. He said he had an odd hunch that Miss Patricia Anderson
Reilly was a home-loving animal and whether she liked it or not he
was going to scent her out, hound her down and run her to earth.
Just a silly play on words, but he did seem confident.

'Don't be so edgy, Boris.' His eyes were glued to the notes and his whole body appeared tense. 'You look as if finding the woman was a matter of life and death.'

'Perhaps it is, so let me concentrate for a minute.' Paddy Reilly, he thought. Born in Castle Landon and Grant considered they might be distantly related. Mother's name Anderson . . . a lover of dogs and horses and a student of zoology . . . Judging from Grant's photograph a hard and determined person who would tolerate only a job she really enjoyed.

Anderson, a home lover and a lover of animals, born in Castle Landon. The facts that had promoted Eric Paulson's hunch were fitting together. That hunch appeared to have failed and Paulson decided to abandon the assignment. He had been a free agent with the right to do that, but Boris was not free. He had to find that woman and must clutch at any straws that came his way.

Obviously Miss Reilly had changed her name unofficially and people usually assume names that come easily to them. People return to places where they were born, as well. Also, a passion for animals is an enduring emotion.

'You are sure that Paulson used those actual expressions, "hound her down" and so on, Ruth? That he used the full name "Patricia Anderson Reilly"?'

'Quite sure, but what is important about that? Eric told Grant he was considering dropping the case, so his hunch didn't come off.'

'Perhaps he didn't pursue the theory doggedly enough.' The tension had left him and Boris looked almost cheerful. 'But I'm going to follow it right through and if his hunch was correct, I'll buy you a dog, Ruth; a great, big Russian borzoi. Now, I'd better try to have a word with Grant. If he's available you can get to work and start to earn the reward he promised Paulson. Miss Reilly had a passion for animals and I want to know if that devotion continued. I'll have some classified directories sent up for you and you can find out whether Paulson's lead pays off.'

He lifted the telephone and grinned. 'Make a list of every pet shop, and veterinary surgeon, every stables and kennels within fifty miles of Castle Landon; all the establishments dealing with

domestic animals, in fact. Then ring them and ask for Miss or Mrs
Patricia Anderson.'

*

Like Sir Ernest Grant, Miss Elizabeth Stapelton was in business and she owned things. The St Michael Social Club in Silver
Street, two blocks of tenements by the river, an antique shop in
Station Parade, a freehold house in one of Daneville's better-class
areas, and thirty thousand pounds' worth of short-term government stocks and blue-chip securities. Now, her possessions had
been increased by tokens for one pound seven and sixpence at the
Golden Fleece public house.

Music, lovely gleaming music. As often happened the jackpot
had come up for her and Lizzie Stapelton pressed a button on the
fruit machine and the counters came rattling out looking as bright
as golden sovereigns. She checked the amount methodically; 'Take
care of the pence and the pounds will take care of themselves' was
a favourite saying of hers and she carried the hoard over to the bar,
smiling smugly as she passed a man who had just lost ten shillings
on the machine.

'Another sweet Cinzano please, Helen, and credit the rest to my
off-licence account.' Miss Stapelton begrudged paying three shillings for a glass of vermouth when one could buy a whole bottle
for a guinea, but though she kept herself to herself, she liked the
Fleece.

'Thanks, dear.' She took her drink back to the corner table, lit
a cigarette, and studied her fellow customers. An elderly married
couple who hadn't spoken a word to each other for the last fifteen
minutes, a courting couple holding hands, three lads in overalls –
one of them was getting a bit tight – and the man on his own who
had lost half a quid. He looked as if he'd lost his wife or his job or
his health, too. Most likely the job because there had been a hint
of desperation in the way he'd tugged at the machine's handle and
now he was staring at his almost empty glass of beer as if longing
to have it refilled.

Probably a smalltime salesman who'd fallen down on his orders
and been given the boot. Miss Stapelton prided herself on being a

judge of character, because also like Sir Ernest, she owned people as well as things. Her immigrant tenants might sleep four to a room and pay through the nose for the privilege, but they were loyal to the core and had damn well better be. Half of them had entered the country without permits and she had a couple of good pals in the police who might hear about it, if necessary. Old Tambi would have some grovelling to do should his nephew fall short on deliveries when the *Daneville Warrior* docked next Thursday.

Miss Stapelton sipped genteelly at the vermouth, enjoying the drink, the atmosphere of the pub and her own thoughts, because she liked to think of people grovelling. 'Please . . . please, mem-sahib, don't turn us out. My wife, so sick, so weak after the last baby. I promise Hussein will bring more this voyage . . . much more.'

Hussein had better bring more, or a lot of people were going to be unhappy. Tambi himself and twelve of her other tenants, the kids at the social club, the woman who did her cleaning, the manager of the antique shop and Elsa Kahn, the exchange student from Hamburg. They were her chattels, she owned them body and soul and she had paid for their loyalty.

Reefers came first. 'Don't worry, dear. In the East people smoke hemp all the time, so of course they can't hurt you.' Then barbi-turates. 'Why, these little blue fellows are medically prescribed for slimming and quite harmless: I use them myself.' Finally she handed out a syringe, the main-line treatment commenced and the fools were hers for life.

Not that they lived or remained useful for very long. That was too much to be expected, but there were always replacements to be found. Little Elsa was her latest acquisition and, though she might not make old bones, the child had turned out to be a real treasure. 'Please, Miss Stapelton, I can't pay you till the end of the month, but I must have a fix. I must . . . must . . . must . . .'

Well, Elsa had had her fix, but her benefactress did not believe in outstanding debts and she was paying for it right now. Lizzie Stapelton looked at the bar clock. Mahomet Achmet was said to take his pleasures vigorously and seventeen stone of sweating black flesh was probably pounding away on top of Elsa at this very moment. Tomorrow there'd be the old socialist alderman for her to entertain, and after him the Dutch sea captain who was impotent till he'd had a brisk half-hour session with the dog whip. Poor little Elsa! But fair is fair. 'Take what you want,' said God. 'Take what you want and pay for it.'

Strange what sort of things gave men a kick, Miss Stapelton thought. She was fifty-six years old but had remained a virgin and the idiosyncrasies of sex puzzled her. That mad killer, Harry Alban, for example. What made him tick? No rape, no interference at all. Just a knotted tie to crush the throat, a strong pull and it was all over. How could that give anyone pleasure?

Personally she did not believe Alban had committed this local murder, whatever the papers might say. Though he looked a commonplace sort of chap, the police must have picked him up if he was wandering around in Daneville. Somebody had had a down on that Mrs Forester and used Alban's method to divert suspicion from himself. Alban was either hiding out in the country around Seamont or safely tucked away with the people who had sprung him. She could hazard a guess as to who they might be. A madman who killed for the fun of it would be a valuable asset to a gang of protection racketeers. Rivals would think twice about muscling in and club owners pay up promptly if their wives, or sisters, or mothers were promised a visit from the Hangman.

But time was getting on and the room had become a bit crowded for her taste. Though the sad man had left the bar and was walking slowly past her towards the door, a group of students had come surging in and they were all talking at the tops of their voices. Miss Stapelton disliked noise and she finished her drink and crossed over to the fruit machine to invest a final sixpence for the road. Obediently the wheels turned and three oranges clicked into line. She scooped up the discs and laid them on the counter.

'Another four bob to go down in the book, Helen. I just can't lose tonight.' She smiled a goodbye and walked out. A small, trim middle-aged woman in a grey tweed costume, matching grey shoes and accessories, and with little, sharp eyes set close together beneath her neat grey hair.

Though the rain had stopped, which was a blessing, the street was almost deserted for the time of night. The scare story that the escaped strangler was in the district had probably kept people indoors. Fools! The poor loony was either starving in a ditch near the prison or comfortably installed in some thieves' kitchen. Even if he was in Daneville, she'd like to see him try anything on her. Her handbag bulged with the antique shop's takings, and above the roll of notes and cheques lay the heavy steel dart which she carried for protection. She'd bought it when she was a girl and made use of it more than once. Twenty years ago, a drunk had tried to molest her and he'd never seen out of his left eye again. Mad Hangman, indeed! Lizzie Stapelton could take care of herself.

It was a gloomy evening. Dank and depressing with mist drifting up from the canal and the lights of Allied House appeared blurred and distorted through the sodden air. For a moment she considered hailing a taxi and then shrugged and turned down the alley beside the pub. She didn't believe in wasting money and her house was only a few minutes' walk away.

Miss Stapelton strode briskly along thinking of profit and loss. Elsa's earnings and the cost of the heroin that Hussein would deliver next Thursday. Her well-polished shoes clicked sharply, a radio blared from an open window and a ship's siren bellowed from down river. She never heard the quiet footsteps coming behind her with long, easy strides that far outpaced her own. She was almost half-way along the alley when something tinkled on the paving stones and she stopped and looked down.

What had she dropped? A disc from the fruit machine that she'd slipped into her pocket and forgotten about? No, it was a shilling. Miss Stapelton stooped and reached out for the coin that had been thrown by the man behind her and it was the last object that she ever did see. The grey of the night changed to bright scarlet, the radio music became a series of hammer blows pounding her head, and though she tried to grab the dart, the handbag had grown too heavy for her to hold. It fell beside the shilling and then there was no colour and no sound. No sensation at all except agonizing pain as her lungs fought for air and the knotted necktie bit deeper and deeper into her throat.

Chapter Seven

Though Ernest Grant rarely attended places of worship, George was right in considering him a religious man, and he was thinking about the supernatural while he listened to Boris.

Did an after life exist and, if so, what was in store for him, he wondered? A glimpse of God's face as he died and eternal peace? Or complete rejection, because his sin had been directed against the Holy Ghost and God had turned away from him for ever?

Hard practice in business, the domination of subordinates like this man, Orel, did not trouble his conscience in the slightest. He had the parable of the unjust steward and the words of the trusting centurion to reassure him on that score. 'I say unto one, Go, and he goeth; and to another, Come, and he cometh.' But evil done to a child would never be forgiven and Paddy had almost been a child when he injured her.

'It were better for him that a millstone were hanged about his neck, and he cast into the sea.' His parents had been strict noncon-formists and texts were displayed everywhere in the house. Grant had put them out of his mind when he grew up, but since Madge's death and his stroke, the memories of childhood terrors kept coming back to him. Sometimes at night he could see the words glowing and writhing like flames at the end of his bed. 'The mills of God grind slowly, but they grind exceeding small.' His rational mind might tell him that the concept of an unforgiving God was ludicrous, that there was no such thing as hell and damnation. But he couldn't really be sure, so he had to find Paddy. He had to receive forgiveness from her. Surely she would show him compassion. They had loved each other so much, once. They had believed they might be related by blood as well as affection, and certainly they were two of a kind in character. He must talk to Paddy and make her forgive him. That was the only way to placate God and gain salvation.

'I have no objection to paying Mrs Renton the same sum that I

promised Paulson, Orel.' The old man had noted everything Boris
had told him and his expression gave no hint of the fears racking
his mind. 'Her greed and lack of public spirit have put me in her
debt already. If the newspapers got hold of the story that I had
employed a private investigator to find Paddy, she would be fore-
warned and your task might become much harder. I would also be
treated as a laughing-stock.

'Five thousand pounds for Mrs Renton and complete security
for you, Orel. Those are the rewards of success, but I'm going to
put a time limit on the assignment. Paddy must be found within
one month from today.' He moved across to a calendar and circled
the date in red pencil. 'I don't have to remind you of the price of
failure, do I, my boy? A one-way ticket back to the Soviet Union
and a punishment which I suspect you most richly deserve.' He
noted the flush of anger on Boris's face and gave a humourless
smile.

'Yes, it was most fortunate that Mrs Renton turned out to be
a go-getter and kept her mouth shut. Not that the information
would have helped the police. The murderer obviously removed
all Paulson's recent files to confuse matters and Paddy's happened
to be amongst them. My business had no connection with the
murder. I'm quite certain of that now.'

'You say "now", Sir Ernest. Did you once suspect that there was
a connection?'

'I'm afraid I did, Orel.' Grant lowered himself into his chair.
'George is bitterly opposed to my finding Paddy because he thinks
I might injure her again if she still refused to forgive me. When I
heard that Paulson had been murdered I got it into my head that
he might have been responsible. But there's no fool like an old fool
and I was quite wrong. My poor George wouldn't have the deter-
mination to kill anybody, however much he wants to protect me
from myself.' The old man's voice became compassionate.

'George is a mixed-up chap and my wife and I are mainly to
blame. Madge was a good woman, but she resented not having
a child of her own and never gave George much attention. He
wanted love, but all he got was a succession of nursemaids till we
packed him off to boarding school. Perhaps that's the reason why

he helps other lame dogs now; felons and maladjusted children.'

'But what about you, sir?' Boris might loathe Ernest Grant, but his personality fascinated him. 'Didn't you show George affection?'

'Precious little, I'm afraid. I knew Madge was jealous of the boy and I respected her feelings; about the only thing in which I did respect them. Besides, when we adopted George, the slump was just over and I was working myself blind to get the firm rolling again.'

Grant sat staring around the room, obviously talking as much to himself as to Boris. 'Yes, the order books were filling up, but we'd come through a bad time, all right. Mines closed, factories working on short-time and the ships rotting at their moorings. In those days a chief officer would count himself lucky to be signed on as a deck hand.

'But it was the ships and the tail-end of the Spanish Civil War that had saved us from liquidation. We fitted out the three fastest we had; the *Daneville Explorer*, the *Daneville Lass* and the *Danecrest*, and sent them off to run Franco's blockade of the Med.'

'You sold arms to Spain, sir?'

'Arms! Don't be a fool.' He growled contempt at the question. 'We'd no money to buy guns or ammunition, but there was something just as profitable and we could get it for a song. The Spaniards were being strangled for lack of fuel, but over here it was going begging. Those ships carried coke to Valencia.

'Yes, that's what brought Aly through the depression; coke to Valencia. There's rather a pathetic ring about the words, I always think. Men risking their lives to take a dull, commonplace substance to a city with such a very beautiful name. Seems to sum up my career in a way. A long fight for money and authority and just one glimmer of romance that went sour.' He closed his eyes for a moment and when he opened them became brusque and business-like again.

'We're wasting time, though. You have only a month to find Paddy and you know what will happen should you fail. It will be home, sweet home, my boy.' Grant's maudlin mood had vanished as he read Boris's thoughts because he loved, not only power, but the risks that went with it. Boris Orel longed to kill him, he was quite certain of that, but a sheet of paper in a bank vault held him prisoner as effectively as the safe that had caged Paulson. Boris was his man and very soon he would lead him to the one person he really wanted to control. Paddy Reilly, whose love he must win back.

'You said you had some questions to ask me, so let's hear them.'

'Before Mrs Renton left for France, Paulson implied that he had a hunch he was on Miss Reilly's trail. Since he told you that he might be going to drop the case, the hunch apparently came to nothing, but I have to follow up every possible lead.' Boris handed him the notes he had made. 'Do you think this suggestion is at all feasible?'

'Anderson?' Sir Ernest had put on his spectacles. 'Paddy was certainly devoted to her parents; used to write to them once a week, and she might have taken her mother's name, I suppose. And Paulson appeared to think she could have returned to Castle Landon or somewhere around these parts. Unlikely, I would imagine. If she changed her name to avoid me, she'd hardly have settled in a place where I might bump into her. Paddy had reason to be frightened of me in those days. I don't know what came over me when she said she'd go to Madge and tell her about us. Then again in the restaurant, I really might have killed her if we'd been on our own.' He shook his head as he read on. 'Whenever I'm in London I go to that restaurant, Orel. A sort of pilgrimage, you might say.

'All the same, we'll consider the possibility that Paddy may have returned north at some time in her life. She loved the country round here; the moors in particular. Couldn't stand London, and gave up the university as soon as we started living together and I asked for a transfer back to Daneville. But when the transfer was offered, there was a string attached with the Chairman's daughter at the end of it.

'I'd known Madge for years and she bored me stiff, but I had to choose between her and Paddy, and the devilish thing is that it only took me seconds to make up my mind. I walked back to the flat and all I could think about was how to break the news to Paddy gently.' He got up and paced the floor with the notes in his hand.

'What's this? You wonder if she might be working for some establishment connected with animals.' Grant turned a page and he was clearly excited. 'It's a long shot, but Paddy was crazy about dogs and horses. She used to go riding in Richmond Park every Sunday whatever the weather was like. As for dogs, she worshipped the brutes and said she couldn't live without one. Even in our little London flat she had one. A smelly mongrel bitch called Patch which snapped at me more than once. I hated the thing, but it was a question of "Love me, love my dog", and I had to pretend that I liked it. Paddy sat up for two nights when Patch was sick and it always slept under our bed. Even when we made love, I could hear that stinking cur wheezing away beneath us. After the brute was killed, I had to fight not to show my true feelings. Yes, you're a clever chap, Orel, and I'm pleased with you. Follow up that animal notion, because it's a real possibility.'

'How did the dog die?' Grant looked up from the notes at Boris's question. 'Every evening Paddy used to take Patch out into the street for the brute to do her business, and a car ran over her. The driver didn't stop and the police considered he must have been drinking. All very sad for Paddy, and it only happened a few weeks before I left her, as well.'

'How much, Sir Ernest?'

'I don't understand.' Grant raised his eyebrows. 'You mean how much had the driver had to drink? Why should I know? I told you that the car didn't stop. Ah, I see.' With a resigned gesture he shrugged his shoulders and laid down the notes. 'You really are smart, Orel. You can read me like a book. I never knew the driver's name. He was just a chap I got talking to in a pub and he said he was down on his luck. Ten pounds was what I paid him; a fair sum of money in those days. I'll regret what I did till my dying day, possibly much longer than that, but at the time . . .' He averted his face so that Boris could not see his expression.

'I heard a scream, I heard a thud and I looked out of the window. I don't think I have ever felt so free, so happy and triumphant as when I saw Paddy kneeling in the gutter beside that hideous, mangled carcass.'

'No, madam, there is nobody named Anderson here.' Ruth apologized, rang off, and consulted her list. That was the thirty-eighth call she had made and she was beginning to believe that Boris's hopes would prove as fruitless as Eric Paulson's, whatever they might have been. Certainly the task was becoming monotonous, and judging by the number of establishments in business, the area must be teeming with animal lovers.

Veterinary surgeons and free clinics, riding schools, hackney stables and pony-trekking clubs, dog breeders, boarding kennels and pet shops. At first she had relieved the tedium by inventing reasons for contacting Miss Anderson should she get through to her, and each number on her list had a note regarding the nature of the establishment as stated in the directories. She needed a vet for a sick cat, she wanted a riding school to give her lessons, she intended to buy a dog. But as the blanks mounted up frustration had increased and the telephone resembled an instrument of torture as she dialled another number.

'Miss Anderson? The lady works or used to work in a surgery near here, you say.' The helpful voice on the line paused in thought. 'Not with us, I'm afraid, but why not try Mr Smith? He's just down the road in Larkfield Drive.'

Ruth replaced the telephone and lit a cigarette before making a further attempt which she felt sure would come to nothing. Her list was shortening; disregarding numbers that had not replied, less than twenty were left, and her only nibbles turned out to be a couple of red herrings. A pet shop in the centre of Castle Landon did employ a Miss Anderson, but her Christian name was Mary, she was sixteen years old and had recently arrived from Connemara. The second hopeful number had been displayed in a large advertisement panel stating that 'The Northmoorland College of Equitation' provided beginners' schooling by skilled horsewomen, and the full finesse of the art demonstrated by ex-cavalry officers. Its phone had rung for a long time before a loud and arrogant voice with a rasping foreign accent had answered.

'Most certainly the lady in question is on my staff and would be happy to arrange a course of instruction for you, Mrs Renton. However, madame is engaged at the moment, so you may discuss your requirements with me personally.' Ruth's soaring hopes crashed to earth when he announced with pride. 'I am her husband, Jan Ignace Andrestan, principal of this college and sometime colonel of cavalry: Polish army.'

'The Dog's Holiday Hotel': no joy. 'The Bankside Pet Shop': no reply. Time was getting on and many of the shopkeepers had not answered their phones. She had noted the numbers to be rung in the morning, but she was sure it would be an equally fruitless task, and she frowned wearily around Boris's office as failure followed failure. The books on the shelves were all of a technical nature, and only the little gilt icon added a personal touch of its occupant.

'The West Hill Peke Breeders' Association' drew blank; 'The Poodle Groomers' did not answer. She and Boris would have to think up some better detective work than this. 'The Riverview Kennels', Castle Landon.

'09-34 5672.' The last digit had twirled into position and almost immediately a woman repeated the number. Somewhere near by a dog was barking and Ruth raised her voice to make the question clear. The instrument almost fell from her hand when the answer came. 'Yes, this is Paddy Anderson speaking.'

Chapter Eight

The murderer had made no attempt to conceal Miss Stapelton's body and it was discovered within half an hour of her death. By sunrise next morning, Daneville resembled a city at war.

The police were out in force everywhere; tired and ill-tempered men, some of them, who had been roused from their beds while off duty. Nobody shared Elizabeth Stapelton's doubts about Harry Alban now. The Hangman was on the rampage, he had killed five times and she and Mrs Forester were in the morgue to prove it. They had both been strangled in the same manner, both bore a close physical resemblance to his three earlier victims, and that was enough. Listening to the radio news and shaking its head over the morning paper the whole town agreed that there would be little sleep for anybody till Alban was caught.

Not only the local police were looking for him. Reinforcements had been hurried in from other areas and the chief constable had requested help from the military. The hotels and boarding houses had already been checked, and before the day was out, every factory and warehouse, every empty building, every ship in the docks, every possible hiding-place would be searched. In the streets any men looking at all like Alban were being stopped and asked for proof of identity. A tall order because, apart from his bulk, there was nothing distinctive about the murderer's appearance, but it had to be done. A crazed animal was running amok and there were only two questions to answer. When would he be caught, or when would they find the body of another victim?

'Very well. On your way, then.' A police sergeant came round from the boot of the car, handed the keys back to Boris and waved him on impatiently. He and his squad were stationed at the motorway approach with orders to stop and search every closed van and one car and open lorry out of five. Like many of his colleagues the sergeant had been about to go off duty when the murder was reported and he had been on his feet for the last six hours. They felt like lead weights as he and an armed plain-clothes man trudged round to the back of the next vehicle. It was a big furniture pantechnicon and both men tensed while the driver pulled open the doors, half-hoping, half-dreading to see the crazed killer crouched to spring from some hiding-place amongst the load. Their torches probed around chairs and tables and bedsteads and other sundry items of a home in transit, and the sergeant finally nodded and gave the automatic dismissal. 'Very well. On your way, then.'

'You don't like the police much, do you?' Ruth watched Boris's face while he switched on the engine and let in the clutch. When they had started out for Castle Landon, he had appeared excited, almost happy and he had reason to be. They both had, if it came to that. The woman she had talked to on the telephone yesterday evening had called herself *Paddy* Anderson, and she sounded middle-aged. Surely she and Miss Reilly must be the same person. If that was the case, she would be five thousand pounds better off and Boris would have earned his employer's good graces. Though she still did not know why, Ruth was certain he was desperate to do that.

But when they had been flagged down at the check point and the sergeant had peered into the car and asked for the keys, she had seen his hand tremble as he held them out and his expression reveal tension. 'From the way you looked just now, one would have thought they were after you instead of that maniac.'

'Was it as bad as that?' The motorway signs appeared and Boris swung into the outside lane. 'No, I don't dislike the police; not the British police. I try not to, that is, but old memories die hard, my dear. Remember that I lived under a dictatorship for most of my life.'

'I suppose it's understandable.' Ruth pulled out her cigarettes. 'But it's two years since you left Russia and this is a free country, not a dictatorship. There is no reason to worry about the police unless you're a criminal or a drunken driver.'

'Hardly the last at this time of the day.' He smiled as she lit a cigarette for him and placed it between his fingers. 'But everybody has something to worry about and most of us have done one criminal action. What about yourself, Ruth? Concealing evidence in a murder case, for instance.' He dragged at the cigarette and relapsed into silence watching the road and the Pennine hills spread out before them.

It was somewhere along this motorway that Lady Grant had died, he remembered as the car roared beneath a bridge. She drank a lot, that was common knowledge in the firm; once she had collapsed at an office party, and they had found a lot of alcohol in her body after the accident. Had she drunk to escape, perhaps? She must have known that Grant had married her for a seat on the board, but believed that one day she could win his love. When Madge Grant realized that she was wrong had alcohol become a poor substitute for love, and on that last drive had the sense of failure started to boil up till there was only one escape from it? A twist on the wheel, the bridge hurtling towards her and 'Goodbye, my love . . . Goodbye, Deadly Earnest.'

If that was the truth Boris did not blame her and not long ago he had leaned out of the window and contemplated suicide himself. But how strange women were. How could anyone really love Ernest Grant? The man might feel guilt now, but the story of the dog proved him a monster and he could imagine how he would have held the weeping girl in his arms and comforted her. 'Poor, poor little Patch, darling. I was so fond of her, Paddy, but please don't cry because you've got me. We've still got each other, Paddy.' Just a few weeks after that Grant beat her up and left her.

And now Sir Ernest wanted to find his Paddy again and the chances were that he would find her; thanks to him. Thanks to Boris Stephanovich Orel, as he called himself. A puppet who obeyed orders however distasteful he found them.

What would happen when they did meet, he wondered? If the woman had changed her name to escape Grant's attentions years ago, if it was she who had replied to his advertisement, she obviously still feared him. Was George right in considering that the old man's remorse and cravings for his lost love showed mental illness and Paddy's rejection might destroy his reason completely? If it were not for the woman's life and a sheet of paper lodged in the bank, that would have been a pleasant possibility. Boris liked the notion of Sir Ernest Grant locked away in an asylum.

'They must be looking for him out here, too.' Ruth considered what she had read about Alban. The car was climbing up into the hills and she pointed to a helicopter circling their flanks. 'Why should Alban have picked this area, Boris? He had no friends or relatives around here. He was a Londoner who had never been in the north of England before his sentence. Yet somebody living in these parts must have arranged his escape and hidden him; must have allowed him to commit those horrible, senseless murders.'

'I don't believe that he was helped to escape or that anybody is hiding him: why should they?' A 'Reduce Speed' sign came into view and Boris edged over into the central lane. 'Alban is not a professional criminal like a forger or a safe-breaker who might be useful to a gang. He had no family, no money and he'd been in prison too long to have outside information to . . . What's the expression? Yes, "turn Queen's evidence" against anybody. Also, a psychopath would be too difficult to control as a strong-arm man.' The right-hand lane was closed now, the traffic slowing to a crawl and police cars were stationed on the verges with roof lights flashing. Once again Boris experienced an absurd feeling of tension, but forced himself to appear normal.

'No, Alban got away on his own and nobody's helping him. It was made clear that Seamont's security arrangements were inadequate, he was wearing normal clothes and he's a fairly ordinary-looking man.' The car in front of them was being flagged down, but a policeman waved Boris on and the road ahead was clear. 'My guess is that he simply hitched a lift on some car or lorry that happened to be coming to Daneville, and judging from these police checks, they believe he's done the same thing again.'

'If he keeps on the move and sticks to big towns it might be days before he's caught.' Ruth wound up her window. The weather had been clear and sunny on the plain, but light mist shrouded the hills and the air had become cold. 'What motivates a man like Alban, Boris? What makes him tick? Ordinary middle-aged women whom he didn't know. That he simply followed and then strangled. No rape, no sexual assault, just the act of killing itself must satisfy him. It's all so crazy, so meaningless.'

'Naturally it's crazy because the man's a lunatic. Alban must have a motive that seems excellent to him, but no rational human being would understand it. Maybe he is possessed, like the maniac in the tombs whose demon was transferred to the animals.'

'The Gadarene swine.' Ruth looked at Boris with astonishment. 'Do you believe in possession? Surely you were brought up as a materialist?'

'Yes, and a very pious one, but Mother Russia with her icons and bearded priests is a dominating old lady and most Slavs are superstitious peasants under the skin. Though religion was frowned upon when I was a boy, it had ceased to be actually forbidden and my parents were very devout. I sometimes think that priests are better than doctors when it comes to probing a human mind.'

'Are your parents still alive, Boris?' Ruth feigned casual interest. 'Did you leave a family behind?'

'No, my mother died during the war and my father was killed in a railway accident five years ago. He was an engine driver and a bridge collapsed under his locomotive.' The exit sign for Castle

Landon slid past and Boris turned into the slow stream. 'There is nobody in Russia who will miss me. But time's getting on, so let's forget Alban and myself and talk about Miss Reilly-Anderson. You told her that we want to buy a dog?'

'Yes, a collie, but there is something else you had better remember. I said we were a childless married couple of three years' standing.' Ruth smiled. 'Don't worry, Boris, I'm not proposing to you, but I thought it was necessary. The Riverview Kennels is most particular, it seems. You can't just go in, pay your money, and walk away with your new-found pal tugging at his lead. They only supply their dogs to breeders, farmers and private families in which one adult member does not go out to work. As I don't imagine I look like a breeder or a farmer, I thought I might as well be Mrs Orel.'

'You'd have done better to have made us Mr and Mrs Smith. You English firmly believe that all foreigners are cruel to animals. The woman's attitude is hopeful, though. Paddy Reilly loved dogs to distraction and this Miss Anderson is determined to see that her dogs get decent homes, so the chances are that they're the same person. But I'll tell you something, Ruth.' The next sign showed that Castle Landon was nineteen miles away and Boris glanced at the dashboard clock. 'I have got to run down this woman and hand her over to Ernest Grant and I intend to do so. But how I hope – how I pray that when we find Miss Reilly we don't start to like her.' A straight dual carriageway lay ahead and he accelerated down it. In less than half an hour they should know whether the future held success or failure: five thousand pounds for Ruth and security for himself. But if success was on the cards, what was in store for little Paddy Reilly?

*

Boris was right in believing that the man the police wanted was alone. He lay stretched out on his back and his eyes flitted around the room that was his hiding-place. He passed his time counting the roses on the faded floral wallpaper, studied the zigzag crack running beside the window, and the waving lines simulating grain on the varnished woodwork, and stared up at the single naked light bulb, sometimes imagining that it was a sun and the room his universe. Occasionally his eyes closed of their own accord, but he always opened them very quickly. His body did not need sleep, and though reality might be boring it was far preferable to daydreams.

The man did not like being alone. He was not gregarious by nature, not a good mixer, but he needed to have people around him so that he could watch their faces, concentrate on what they were saying and nod sagely if a word was addressed to him. When he was on his own the blurred images always started to reappear, and keeping his eyes open didn't really help, because they were lodged behind them deep in his brain.

There were six hundred and forty-three roses on the wall facing him; it had taken five attempts to be sure of the number, and soon he must start to count those on his right. The task seemed endless, but so was the other task that God had given him to do. The man had never heard of Sir Perceval and his quest for the Holy Grail, but if he had, he would have felt a deep kinship with the knight. Like Perceval he was ordained to pursue a dream till the end of his life. The difference between them was that his dream was a nightmare.

He pulled himself up from the bed and looked longingly at the radio on the chest of drawers. Should he turn it on for a short while? There might be music to cheer him up, or a story, or perhaps a quiz programme. He rarely got the answers right, but the concentration took his mind off things, and there were usually jokes between the quizmaster and the competitors. He did like a good joke.

The man crossed over to the chest, reached out to switch on the radio, and then glanced at the alarm clock ticking busily away beside it and drew back his hand. At about this time yesterday he had been listening to the 'Seekers' and very good they were, too. He was enjoying himself, but then there had been a news summary and things were said about him: horrible, unjust things. He couldn't risk hearing them again.

He left the radio and wandered around the room. He examined the gas stove, peered aimlessly at the books on a shelf, and stared at a picture over the mantelpiece. He would have to take it down before he started to count the roses on that wall.

But his air of aimlessness vanished when he reached the wardrobe. Slowly and expectantly like a child about to dip into a bran tub he pulled open the door and his face went rigid as he looked inside. Clothes lay on the hangers, shoes and boots at the base, there was a shelf for socks and handkerchiefs, and almost at eye level the thing that excited him. A little press holding a row of brightly-coloured neckties.

Chapter Nine

'You bully, Rose, you fat, cowardly bully.' The woman was beside herself with fury, the chain swung backwards and forwards in her hand and there was nothing in the world she would have liked better than to lash her assistant across the face with it. 'I'm going to make you a promise, my girl. Your father may own part of this business, you may be bigger and stronger than me, but if I ever see you do anything like that again, I'll give you a thrashing you'll never forget and throw you off the premises.'

'But Nell kept growling at me, miss. I felt she was going to snap when I bent down to take the puppies.' Rose Crichton was a hulking eighteen-year-old, but she was very frightened of Miss Anderson and tears were dribbling down her cheeks. Between the two women the old collie bitch lay stretched out in a straw-lined box with three puppies tugging at her dugs. Though her hackles were down and she appeared placid, her eyes were still watchful. 'I felt I had to teach her a lesson.'

'And by that you mean tying the dog to the wall and flogging her.' Miss Patricia Anderson fought against slashing out with the chain. Though she was a small and slightly built woman her face was flushed beneath her thick make-up and she looked as formidable as a fighting cock. 'My God, it's you that needs a lesson, Rose. If I hadn't stopped you in time, if you had really hurt old Nellie . . .' Her hand tightened around the leather loop and then she drew back. You mustn't hit her, she told herself. Control your temper and don't do anything that might get into the papers, that might give you away. Don't harm yourself for the sake of a lout like Rose Crichton.

To resist temptation Miss Anderson threw the chain on to a bench. Because Rose was too stupid to get into a university, her parents had sent her here; kennel management was regarded as a ladylike occupation these days, and she had taken the girl on as her father was one of the three local businessmen who had invested money in Riverview. But any more trouble and she'd keep her promise and kick the fool out. The kennels were showing an excellent profit, thanks to hard work and careful breeding, and the other shareholders would back her to the hilt.

'You growled because you know that Rose doesn't like you, Nell.' She stooped down and fondled the black-and-white head. 'You were nervous, weren't you, old girl? You thought she was going to steal your puppies and hurt them.'

'But you told me to take the puppies, Miss Anderson.' Rose dabbed her eyes with a grimy handkerchief. 'She hasn't enough milk, and you told me to feed them from the bottle.'

'But I didn't tell you to snatch them away from her, did I?' The dog licked her hand and Miss Anderson's fury started to dwindle. Though she hated children in general and Rose in particular, the girl was strong and willing and it would save a lot of worry if she could train her. She'd had so much worry lately; she just couldn't take any more.

'One must be firm with animals, but gentle, too.' The collie's tail thumped against the box while she removed the rope from its collar. 'Above all, never be frightened of them. Nell could smell your fear and that made her growl. This is the way to take them out.' She slid her hand under one of the month-old puppies and drew it away from the half-moon of the mother's belly. 'You remove the others now, Rose, and I give you my word that Nell won't snap.' She laid the squirming body in a basket and moved aside for the girl to obey her.

'It's all right – quite all right, Nellie dear, nobody is going to harm your babies, and you'll have them back very soon. That's better.' She nodded approvingly as Rose laid the two puppies beside the first. 'Give them a feed with the bottle and then replace them just as gently.' She walked towards the door of the shed and then paused and her voice became harsh again. 'But don't forget my promise. I meant every word I said, because the one thing I just won't tolerate is cruelty to animals.'

It was too nice a day to remain really angry for long, she thought as she stepped into the open air, though the sight of that brainless fool preparing to lash out with the chain had shocked her badly. Not completely brainless, either: Nell was a timid, old dog and Rose would never have dared to hit one of the other brood bitches, whether it was tied up or not.

Patricia Anderson lit a cigarette to calm her nerves and looked out across the municipal park that ran alongside the kennels. The trees were bare of leaves and the autumn flowers coming to the end of their bloom, but it was still a pleasant view and the sky was clear apart from a belt of cloud hanging above the hills to the west. She frowned towards the recent eyesores of a council estate and a shopping parade bordering the main road and shook her head. There had been complaints that her dogs disturbed the tenants, but as the buildings had been put up long after Riverview was established and one of her backers was on the council, she'd ridden out the storm.

And surely the other storm had passed as well? Surely he must have given up hope now and realized he could never get her back. She dragged hungrily at the cigarette recalling the shock of seeing that advertisement in the newspaper with her name and his initials glaring out at her. Half a lifetime had passed, and after all that had happened he wanted to find her again.

Had they ever loved each other? Or had Ernest simply wanted to dominate her, and she been flattered by him till her pride was worn down by his power and drive and self-assurance? But a little pride had remained when he broke the news that he was leaving her; just enough self-respect to prevent her writing to Madge, though he had never realized that. She remembered his expression after she made the threat and how he had screamed as his fists shot out. 'Contact Madge and I'll kill you, Paddy, kill you . . . kill you.'

He was insane, of course. Miss Anderson stroked the scar beneath her make-up. He really would have killed her if the neigh-bours hadn't intervened. She might have died in the restaurant, too. For him to believe that she could forgive him after the way he had treated her, to imagine that she might accept money and become his mistress! She would never forget the grip of his hands around her neck while the coffee dribbled down from his face and the waiters came rushing across the restaurant.

But why think about him? Ernest Grant would never find her and she had thrown away the shame with which he had burdened her. She was free of him and even though he was insane, he must have realized that reconciliation was impossible. Surely he must have given up hope?

Harry Alban. The thought of insanity brought the name into her mind and she looked towards the hills again. Alban: the name of a martyr, of a cathedral city and of a madman whose victims were very much like herself! Small, ageing and defenceless women. Mrs Forester's husband was a cripple and Miss Stapelton had lived alone.

'Pull yourself together, Paddy.' A dog barked and she spoke aloud. It was an unpleasant coincidence that Alban's victims resembled her physically, but too much of a long shot to imagine that their paths might meet. No one knew better than she that miracles did happen at times, but odds like that were out of the question. Besides, Daneville was miles away and she was certainly not defenceless; there were over fifty bodyguards only too ready to protect her. Mott and Lad, the two Welsh sheepdogs, would sleep in the bungalow tonight and if that long shot did come up, it would be the Hangman who got his throat crushed. An absurd precaution, of course. Millions of women shared her physical type and age group and most probably Alban would be under lock and key before nightfall. All the same, if he were still at large, she'd sleep better with Mott and Lad near by.

Paddy Reilly brightened at the thought and she strolled forward between the lines of sheds and wired-in runs, eyeing their occupants with love and professional appraisal, and now and again stopping for a word of greeting.

'Hullo, Shannie, your family are coming along nicely, aren't they? All right, Bob, I know you're pleased to see me, but there's no need to bark your silly head off. Come here and let's have a look at you, Mick.' She stooped and stroked a nose thrust through the mesh. 'Yes, you're a fanatic, aren't you? You've got really crazed eyes that show you're a born worker. And so you should have, boy. Didn't your father win a gold at Aberystwyth last year? In a month or two I'll get fifty guineas for you by just lifting the telephone and you'll be worth a hundred if they train you properly.'

Who could that be? A car had turned into the drive and was drawing up before her bungalow. She frowned and then hurried towards it. That woman with the unusual name who had rung her up last night and her husband, of course. In her fury with Rose she had forgotten all about the appointment. They looked a pleasant enough couple, she thought, watching Boris and Ruth climb out, but she would vet them very carefully. She was always careful with people who wanted to buy a dog as a pet. Her babies only went to homes where they'd get good treatment and plenty of exercise.

'Mr and Mrs Orel?' She held out her hand to Ruth and then to Boris. 'You telephoned me last night about buying a male collie pup?'

'We certainly hope to buy one, Miss Anderson.' Boris bowed as he took her hand and he knew that he was home and dry. The woman's voice was mannish and she wore heavy leather boots, a tweed skirt and jacket, and a roll-neck sweater. Her thick make-up would effectively conceal a scar, her features had not aged well and they bore little resemblance to those of the girl in Grant's photograph. But she was Paddy Reilly all right.

'You have plenty of dogs to choose from, I see.' Their arrival had set up a chorus of barks and Boris smiled towards the rows of pens.

'I have, Mr Orel, and they vary in price from a hundred guineas to ten pounds for the poorer specimens. The last figure may seem high, but it is to protect the runts from being resold for vivisection. But before you inspect any of them, do come inside and have a chat. Your wife told me something of your circumstances, but I don't sell my animals to just anybody and I'd like to have a few more details.' She led the way through the hall of the bungalow to a room serving as both office and parlour. In the centre of the floor a glass-fronted cabinet filled with silver trophies stood like a frontier post dividing two domains. To its right there was a battered oak desk piled with stud books and technical journals, a filing cabinet, and a trestle table supporting veterinary equipment. The walls behind them were almost papered with exhibition awards and pedigree certificates and the general effect was of businesslike untidiness.

But, beyond the cabinet, everything was quite different; chintzy and feminine and so neat and tidy that one felt it would be a crime to tilt a cushion out of place. The whole room had a rather disturbing atmosphere, as though it were used by two temperamentally unsuited strangers.

'You said you have no children, Mrs Orel.' She waved them to a sofa and seated herself at the desk. 'That's in your favour, because children can make an animal's life a misery. There are also callous fools who buy their child a puppy as an animated toy and get rid of it when the brat becomes tired of the poor little devil.' She turned towards Ruth and from the window a beam of sunlight lit up her face. 'And I understand that you have a garden.'

'Quite a large garden.' Ruth smiled because that was only half a lie. She intended to buy a house with a garden in the near future and she could already picture Sir Ernest Grant writing out her cheque. Till a few moments ago she had felt as conscience stricken as Boris by the thought of leading Grant to a woman who was desperate to be left alone. Now, like Boris she had noted a tell-tale feature which not only corresponded with the photograph but drove her guilt away.

In the photograph and viewed briefly, Miss Reilly's face had appeared pleasant enough. But the sunlight showed that the eyes were not merely hard. They were so deep-set that they hardly seemed to belong to her and they looked completely merciless. They made Ruth think of an inquisitor's eyes viewed through the slits of a mask.

Chapter Ten

'Well, that's that. All we need now is a phone box.' They had made their purchase, a six-week-old puppy to be collected after it was weaned in a fortnight, and waved their goodbyes to Miss Anderson. Boris turned the car out into the main road.

'Just one call to Grant and you'll be five thousand pounds richer, Ruth. What does it feel like to have earned that sort of money for a few hours' work?' Personally he felt dirty and full of disgust for himself. Unlike Ruth his sense of guilt had not vanished when he set eyes on the woman, though he suspected that she was a hard and callous person redeemed only by her love of animals. He was also sure that she and Paddy Reilly were one, but habit and caution had forced him to make absolutely certain. He had hated his job during every moment that he prompted her.

Did Miss Anderson travel about the country buying dogs from farmers and other breeders? The question had led them to discuss North Wales, the Scottish border and finally Otterburn, the town from which the reply to Ernest Grant's advertisement had been sent. Boris had claimed a friend in the area and ascertained that she had been there during the week the letter was posted.

What technical knowledge was needed to run a breeding kennels successfully? From this he learned that Miss Anderson had studied zoology when she was young but never taken a degree. The picture was almost complete and the puppy itself had provided the final confirmation.

'Here's the one I fancy, Ruth,' he had said, kneeling before five puppies in a basket. 'This chap with the white patch over his eye. If you feel the same and we buy him, we might call him Patch.' While his hand fondled the little dog's stomach Boris had looked up and seen a flicker that might have been pain in the sharp eyes. The memory of the dog that Ernest Grant had paid ten pounds to have destroyed obviously remained and from that moment he had ceased to think of her as anyone except Paddy Reilly. It was also at that moment that he began to really loathe himself, and he recalled every word of Grant's confession: '. . . felt so free, so happy and triumphant as when I saw Paddy kneeling in the gutter beside that hideous, mangled carcass.'

And now Grant was to be reunited with his Paddy and he and Ruth were responsible. Fate had added another black mark to his record, because even if the woman was as callous as her eyes suggested, surely she was entitled to live her life in peace?

He could imagine how Ernest Grant would make his proposal. 'I still love you, Paddy. I have done you immense harm, and I want to make amends, so please forgive me. Please marry me, darling. There is no need for you to give up your work here if you say yes. Quite the opposite, in fact.' A hint of triumph might appear on the old man's face while his hand produced a document for her examination. 'Your backers were easy men to do business with, Paddy, and I own the controlling interest in Riverview Kennels now.'

And what would happen when the woman refused him? He was quite sure that she would do so. Was George right in believing that Grant would break down and attack her physically as he had done in the past? No, Boris did not believe that a man of Grant's age and position would resort to physical violence, because he would have the means to hurt her much more brutally. 'Do what I say, Paddy. You must do what I ask, because I own this place now. If you refuse I'll close it down and send every blasted dog you have to a medical research centre.'

'I asked how you felt, Ruth?' She had remained silent and Boris repeated the question. Ruth had hardly spoken a word since they got into the car and was sitting slumped sideways in her seat and staring out of the window. 'Elated, or as filthy as I do, my dear? All we have to do is to call my employer and make an appointment for you to collect five thousand quid.' Boris's remorse made him speak bitterly. He himself had no choice in the matter. He had to hand over the woman to Grant, but Ruth was selling her for money. 'Or has the sum dwindled to thirty pieces of silver?'

'It's dwindled to nothing, Boris, and I do feel guilty, but not about Miss Reilly.' She looked up at him as he braked at a roundabout. 'I'd have had no compunction about giving Grant her address, because that woman probably deserves any hell that's going. But there's a phone booth at the end of that lay-by, so pull up and we'll make our call. It won't be to Grant, however, and there'll be no reunion for him or reward for us, I'm afraid. We're going to ring the police, Boris.' She opened her handbag as the car stopped. 'I lied to them because I was quite certain that Eric had not located Miss Reilly and the case had nothing to do with his murder. Now I've been proved wrong and I'll have to take the consequences.' She took a crumpled scrap of paper from the bag and handed it to him.

'There was a jotting pad on her desk and when I was looking at the puppy's pedigree certificate I noticed this entry and tore out the page.'

'I can only ask why.' Boris studied the scribbles and notes. A doodle of a flight of birds, two telephone numbers, and a memo to order some anti-distemper vaccine. 'This means nothing to me, Ruth.'

'There's no reason why it should, but it means a very great deal to me.' Her hair brushed his cheek as she leaned across and pointed to an entry. 'This happens to be the number of Eric's office.'

'God! That shows that he did locate her.' Possibilities and implications raced through Boris's mind. Eric Paulson had found Miss Reilly and realized what his success could mean to her. Like himself, the detective might have felt pity, but he was also a man of business, so had he come into the open and suggested terms? Sir Ernest Grant was prepared to pay five thousand pounds for Miss Reilly's whereabouts. Would she pay him the same amount if he dropped the case and left her in peace?

'It also means that she probably killed him.' Ruth's thoughts were ahead of his. 'That woman struck me as being capable of murder so what would she have done if Eric had offered to drop the case for Grant's fee and she hadn't got the money? I think she'd have gone to his office and tried to stall, probably offering him a down payment in cash and the rest when she had time to borrow or sell securities.

'Eric was a fair man, but he believed in looking after number one and he'd have covered himself by telephoning Grant then and there. He would have said the assignment appeared impossible and he was thinking of dropping it and accepting another if he didn't get a firm lead very soon. That would give Miss Reilly time to raise the money and honour their agreement.' Ruth's eyes were closed and she kept clicking her fingers while she tried to concentrate.

'I can imagine exactly what happened. The woman listening to Eric talking to Grant on the telephone and knowing that she can never find the money in time. When he rings off, she hands over a down payment in notes and watches him open the safe and lean forward to put them in the cash box. Can't you picture her at that moment, Boris? Can't you see those horrible little eyes becoming even sharper when she realizes that there is an escape for her? Just one quick push on the door and her worries are over. Isn't it logical?'

'Perfectly logical, but it will take some proving.' Ruth's own eyes were still closed and Boris pulled out his cigarette lighter. 'If your theory is correct, and most probably it is, Miss Reilly also removed those files and I think it's unlikely that she would have left any fingerprints. All we can show the police is this.' He snapped on the lighter, started to bring the paper towards its flame and then pulled them apart quickly.

What a fool he was. He had been about to destroy the evidence against Miss Reilly because he still thought of himself as a slave condemned to serve his master's interest whatever the cost. But now the chains were broken, the boot was on the other foot, and he had Deadly Earnest by the short hairs. He grinned as the colloquial phrases occurred to him. If he could prove Miss Reilly a killer, Grant would never dare to trouble him any more. In exchange for silence he would be a free man with only his conscience to worry about.

'Boris!' Ruth had opened her eyes, seen the lighter flame, and she snatched the paper away from him. 'You were going to burn this – the only evidence that we can show the police? In God's name, why?'

'Give it back to me, Ruth. I am not going to burn anything, but neither are we talking to the police.' He snapped off the lighter and stuffed it into his pocket. 'We are going to tell Ernest Grant that we have found Miss Reilly and claim our payments.'

'Payments! You must be mad.' He held out his hand for the scribbled page, but Ruth's grip tightened and she drew back. 'I may be greedy and dishonest, but Eric Paulson was always decent to me and I won't be an accessory to his murder. Why do you want to protect the woman, Boris? How much is Grant paying you?'

'A great deal, and I must have that paper, my dear.' Boris's studied English accent vanished and his voice became strident and foreign as she edged still farther away and pushed her hand between the seat and the car door. 'I don't want to hurt you, so please give it to me.'

'No, Boris.' Apart from passing vehicles, the road was deserted. His left hand gripped her shoulder, his right was doubled into a fist, and she could see murder in his face. But though Ruth was desperately afraid she intended to hang on to that flimsy scrap of evidence. She struggled to twist away from him and open the door, felt his fingers dig into her flesh like pincers and covered her face with her arm.

Only one blow came. A short jab below the jaw that sent her sprawling sideways across the seat and would have knocked her unconscious if he hadn't tried to pull back at the last moment. With shock and fear racking her more than the physical pain, she waited for Boris to hit her again and then very slowly lowered her arm.

'Sorry, Ruth . . . so sorry, darling . . . can't ask you to forgive me, but please believe that I am sorry.' His face was turned away from her, but all the aura of menace had vanished.

'This has happened before many, many times, and I am no better than Grant, or that mad strangler, or any pervert who beats women.' His face was still averted and his body appeared to have grown smaller and younger. It almost seemed as if the years had slipped away and there was a boy slumped on the seat beside her. 'But I will never harm you or anyone else again, so go and telephone the police.'

'Not till you tell me why you wanted to protect Miss Reilly, Boris.' She reached out and tilted his face towards hers. 'Just what is the hold Grant has over you?'

'Grant came upon certain information and he has the power to send me back to Russia. A firing squad will be the most tolerable reception I can expect on arrival.' He pushed her hand aside and lowered his face again. 'I had wanted to leave the Soviet Union for a long time, but it was impossible. Then fate came on the scene. Two passengers hijacked a plane flying over East Germany and I tried to overpower one of them and failed. A bullet fractured the rudder control and the aircraft struck a radio tower. Thirty-two people were killed because of my failure, but by a miracle I survived and found myself near the British military mission in West Berlin.' He still spoke as if English was an unfamiliar language and he was searching for every other word.

'When I pulled myself together it seemed as if that miracle had been performed to give me freedom as well as life and I decided to ask for political asylum under the name of a man who had died in the crash. I only used his name and position, because I knew very little about him and I gave the British authorities a factual account of my own parentage and so forth. I just hoped that nobody would ask too many questions and I was right.

'But that was two years ago, Ruth, and fate has changed her mind about me. I was a fool to think I could escape from the past and I must return to Russia and take the consequences. Now, please go and telephone the police.'

'Not till I know everything, my dear. Even if you have a criminal record in Russia, you'd never be deported. You're a British citizen.'

'Who said anything about deportation? Your people would not deport me. They'd regard me as a much more valuable asset than a market adviser.' There was the merest hint of humour in his tone. 'But I shall have to go home as soon as the order arrives. Surely the penny has dropped by now? Nobody cares about the defection of Boris Orel who was a minor expert on economics, but two people in Russia are held responsible for the good behaviour of a man called Boris Dubassof. They would suffer severely if he was found to be alive and failed to obey orders.'

'You mean hostages, Boris?' Ruth laid her hand on his and he did not withdraw it. 'But you told me that you had no family except your father and he died in a railway accident.'

'I said that there was nobody in Russia who would miss me, but I have a family. A wife whose name is Shura and a little girl called Tania. Tania will be three years, eight weeks and five days old now.' He had raised his head slightly as he paused to get the age exactly right and Ruth saw that his lips smiled but his eyes were expressionless. 'My marriage broke up shortly after my daughter was born but though Shura and I ceased to love each other we were forced to remain man and wife for the sake of appearances. Divorce and accommodation are hard to obtain in my country.' Once again there was a trace of bitter humour in his voice. 'All the same I cannot allow them to be punished on my account.

'They won't suffer, however, because what happens to me is unimportant now. I thought I could be reborn as a human being, but by striking you I proved that I was wrong. I am just a . . . a cornered rat; a creature with no right to live and my death will be a simple cleansing operation. Now, please go to that phone box and leave me alone.

'Why did Shura stop loving me? Simply because she is a decent woman and I was a fool. One day I got tired of pretence and told her the truth about myself. How stupid can one get?' He clenched his fist remembering how it had slammed against Ruth's jaw; also remembering the way his wife had looked at him while he made his confession and how she had drawn back as though his breath was poisoned.

'Don't, Boris. Please don't.' His fist had shot out against the speedometer dial and glass lay on the floor and blood dribbled from his knuckles. Ruth grasped the torn hand between both of hers. 'What is the truth, darling? Tell me what you told Shura. Please tell me and I'll try to understand.'

'You understand! You, a little English girl with generations of freedom and security behind her. Slav means *slave*, my sweet, and you wouldn't understand in a thousand years.' He looked at her and laughed. 'All the same I'm tired of lies, tired of running away, so I might as well entertain you for a few minutes. And when I've finished, I want you to get out of the car and make three phone calls.'

He scribbled two numbers on the back of a cigarette packet and handed it to her. 'Advise the police that they'd better look into Miss Reilly's activities, but talk to Grant first, because you might as well collect your reward. Tell him to meet you somewhere in Castle Landon with his cheque made out if he wants the address. It will be amusing if he arrives at the bungalow at the same time as the police.

'The last call is to the Soviet embassy in London. The switchboard usually keeps one waiting, so you may need some loose change.' He rummaged in his pocket. 'Get through to Mr Alexis Tchagin and inform him that Boris Dubassof is alive and may be found at my address. Say that Comrade Dubassof is ready for his orders to return home.

'Now, you want to know why my wife stopped loving me, Ruth. Why no woman can love me and feel clean.' The years started to roll back while he talked. The interior of the car faded and became a room, though the driving mirror remained before his eyes. Boris was a boy again and from the mirror a man's face was watching him.

Chapter Eleven

The man had been waiting for him in the office of Professor Reydkin and there was nothing at all distinguished about his appearance. A mild-looking man of medium height, medium build who was just approaching middle age. His hair had started to recede, he wore a shabby suit with leather-bound cuffs and elbows and he was smoking a pipe and obviously not enjoying it. He appeared somewhat prim and old-maidish, and Boris fancied he was a junior lecturer till he dismissed Reydkin with a curt word of thanks and sat down behind his desk.

'Please take that chair, Boris Dubassof,' he said, nodding affably before opening a report sheet. 'My name is Vanin . . . Peter Ilyich Vanin and unknown to you I have been taking a close interest in your career.' His pipe was not drawing well and he seemed to have difficulty in even keeping it alight.

'You are a bright fellow, it seems, Dubassof. Your teachers state that your academic progress is excellent and you are a keen athlete. You also attend night classes to study English, German and Italian. All very commendable.'

'Thank you, comrade.' Boris now imagined that he was some benevolent inspector from the Bureau of Higher Education, but in this also he was quite wrong.

'You have yourself to thank, Boris Stephanovich, and there is something else in your favour. You are not only popular with your teachers and fellow students, but you have the type of personality which makes people eager to confide in you ... to discuss their problems and hopes freely. That is a very, very valuable asset, indeed.

'Curse this thing.' Vanin had given up his battle with the pipe and he laid it down. 'My wife keeps nagging that I smoke too many cigarettes and I've been trying to compromise, but it's no use. I'm a wet smoker and I just can't get on with a pipe at all.' He took a packet of long-funnelled *Mockbas* from his crumpled jacket and lit one with relish.

'Now, what was I coming to? Yes, your future intentions which are to enter the planning department of the State Railways. How will a knowledge of foreign languages help you there, Dubassof?'

'Railways cross frontiers, comrade, so they are bound to be international. Also foreign techniques have to be studied and sometimes adopted.'

'Fair enough, but what about your reasons for choosing a railway career? Aren't they rather emotional?' Vanin pushed aside the file and spoke from memory. 'Your father is a locomotive engineer and you are very close to each other. That is perfectly natural because your mother was murdered in Germany when you were very young. But it is not natural or desirable that you should feel emotionally forced to follow in your father's footsteps. By the way, I hope that Stephan Feodorovich is in good health. They discovered a slight cardiac murmur during his last medical.'

'He was well enough when I last heard from him, comrade.' Though Vanin could not have spoken more pleasantly, Boris found the line of questioning disturbing.

'Excellent. Let us hope he remains so.' Vanin blew cigarette smoke through his nostrils and watched it drift to the ceiling. 'Since leaving home you correspond regularly with your father each week. That pleases me because I have two children of my own. I hope we will remain as close as the years go by ... as concerned for each other's welfare. But do relax and stop calling me comrade at every sentence, Boris. That formality is out of date and I have your future very much at heart. I also hope that before long you will come to regard me as a friend. Ah, here is your letter stating why you feel cut out for a railway career.'

He unclipped it from the report form and shook his head. 'You made a good case, Boris, but I can read between the lines. Childhood memories, filial ties and sentiment are your true motives. I suppose that when you were young your father let you ride on the footplate with him now and again.'

'Many times, but I have thought things out very carefully and I am sure my choice is correct.'

'Many times! He was obviously no respecter of regulations.' A tongue clicked in mock disapproval. 'No, you are still a boy with romantic notions, Boris, and your talents are not going to be wasted on the railways. The state knows better and it has other plans for you.' Vanin crumpled the letter into a ball and threw it towards Reydkin's waste-paper basket. It missed and he smiled wryly. 'A poor shot, but I am better with other missiles.' In spite of the smile, Boris sensed that there was something rather sinister about his mild, friendly face.

'When I was about your age, I also imagined that I knew what I wanted. I was training to be a teacher: I longed to teach more than anything on earth and I believed that I was completely cut out for the job.' He fondled the pipe with small, well-manicured fingers that a woman might have envied. 'But I was persuaded that I was mistaken, just as I have to persuade you, Boris. The individual rarely knows what is best for him. That may not be true about other races, of course, but we are Russians who rely on the judgment of the Party and our leaders, and before the revolution we obeyed the Tsars. A sheep-like people who follow blindly.'

'What career have you in mind for me, then?' Boris had eyed him with astonishment. Stalin was in power, Beria's secret police were feared like the plague and there might be a concealed microphone in the office. By coupling the Party with the Tsars as instruments of coercion, the man had committed something akin to blasphemy.

'One which I suspect you will neither like nor approve of at first, but you will become resigned to your duties in time. Some people even enjoy the work, though I am glad to say that I am not one of them. However, like a street-sweeper's, it is necessary work and without it the system would melt away as quickly as that snow.' He pointed towards the window and the white flakes shimmering on the Kremlin towers.

'A few of us do break, naturally. A man of my acquaintance committed suicide only last month. He was a selfish, unthinking fool and his widow was executed yesterday morning. That shocks you, doesn't it?' Vanin smiled at the disgust on Boris's face. 'But she had to die as a warning to other husbands. We usually find that family men are more reliable. You yourself have an affectionate disposition; your relationship with your father proves that, and you will be expected to marry after your training. When that happens I would advise you not to discuss your occupation with your wife. Women are not always as understanding as one would like them to be.' He shrugged resignedly, took a final pull at the cigarette and stubbed it out.

'Your training will be very thorough and helpful, that I can promise you. After finishing your degree course here, you will go to another school to be taught the tricks of your trade and something that is far more important. You will be shown how to live without mercy, Boris. You will cast out compassion and become a completely emotionless instrument of power.' His voice rose to a sudden bitterness, and though Boris was stunned by the realization of what was in store for him, he also realized that he was looking at one of the most distressed human beings he had ever seen. Peter Vanin's own training had failed, he hated his job, but he had a family to think of.

'I am sorry, Boris, but you have no say in the matter.' He took an identity card from his pocket. 'You have been selected and that is that. If you value the well-being of your father, you must just accept the situation.' Vanin leaned across the desk and held out the card. It showed his photograph with an embossed seal blurring the forehead like a burn or a birthmark, and four lines of print stating his name and age, the fact that he had a bullet scar on his left shoulder and the position he held. 'Screening Officer – Department of Internal Security – Answerable only to Marshal Lavrenti Beria in person.'

'That's all there is to tell, Ruth. The secret police trained me well and I became an efficient instrument of oppression.' The images had faded and Boris's own face was reflected back at him from the driving mirror.

'I suppose I might have refused if it hadn't been for the threat against my father. At least I hope I would have had the courage. I hated every filthy aspect of the work, but I was trapped. Before my father died they made me marry and I had Shura and then Tania to consider. Even when I had told Shura what I was and she turned away from me, I couldn't let them down, and I still can't. After that aircraft crashed I imagined that I could escape without endangering them but what a bloody fool I was.' He took care not to look at Ruth's face, knowing the contempt he was bound to see on it. The same expression that his wife had worn after he made his confession to her.

'Grant stumbled upon my false identity by chance, and even if I do what he wants, his hold over me will remain. There's no point in my running away any more. It would only prolong the agony, so go and telephone, Ruth. I have to return to Russia and there is no punishment that my servility hasn't earned me. God, the things they made me do! I have provoked confidences and then informed against men and women who trusted me. I have spied on people who regarded me as a friend and colleague: my last assignment was to watch over that party in the plane. It is ironic to think that the hijackers died and I was the only one who got away.' Again he clenched his fist and drove it against the dashboard.

'Those were my more innocent duties, though. Would you like to hear how a man's spirit can be broken, Ruth? The interrogations under the bright lights, the cells where the temperature keeps varying from intense heat to bitter cold, the primitive beatings and the sophisticated injections of sodium pentothal. Did you know that the knout is the only whip that cuts in exact parallel lines?' Apart from one question Ruth had been sitting in complete silence since he began his story and Boris's voice became savage. 'But I won't disgust a civilized English woman with more details, so go and make those phone calls. Just get it over and done with.'

'Very well.' She climbed out of the car and he watched her

walk very slowly towards the booth. She seemed to have trouble in pulling back the door, as though its spring was almost too strong for her, but in time she managed and he saw her dial a number.

He had no regrets, he knew that he had made the right decision. He might have taken that paper from Ruth by force and told her nothing, but the fact that he had struck her proved that he had remained a monster. He would pay for his past by going back to Russia to face a traitor's death. There was no future for him and he would die like Peter Vanin, his tutor. A poor comparison because Peter had died honourably. He had crunched cyanide when the British intelligence men arrested him, but many men had bad deaths. He had once been told how Lavrenti Beria had died after the bullets thudded into him. That tight, oval face which resembled a rubber inner tube stretched over the bone structure, split open in a scream as he stared down at his torn belly. And tears – real tears had appeared from under the rimless glasses while the little fountains of blood and urine spurted between his clutching fingers. Beria had been the most hated man in Russia, but Boris could have forgiven him anything except the thought of that rubber face weeping.

Soon it would be his turn to show if he could die decently, but how he wished he could choose the manner of dying, because there were so many easy ways to go. He looked at the ignition key and thought of a few of them. A speeding car had given Lady Grant peace, there was the clean air between a high window and the ground, a bullet, or the soft mud of a river in which a man could hide.

Easy death was not for him, however. Soon the police would ask a lot of questions. They would want to know why Ernest Grant had employed him as his agent and Grant might tell them. If that happened, his identity would be made public and the Soviet embassy staff read newspapers. They also regarded suicide as a crime and Shura and Tania would pay for his treason. He had to accept what was in store for him and he had witnessed a number of executions. Quite oblivious of time, or the sound of passing traffic, or the sunlight on the windscreen Boris laid his forehead against the steering wheel and waited for Ruth to return.

'You got through to all of them?' He looked up as the door opened and she climbed in beside him. 'You spoke to Alexis Tchagin in person?'

'I'll tell you what I've done, Boris, but do get that expression of Slavonic agony off your face, because I'm in no mood for Dosto-evsky at the moment. Nor am I in the mood to talk to the police, so give me a cigarette in return for this.

'I said that I wanted a cigarette, Boris.' She had held out the page from Miss Reilly's jotting pad, but he looked completely indif-ferent as though he had forgotten what it was. 'The only person I've talked to is Ernest Grant. We're meeting him at five o'clock and I've promised to take him to his dear, darling Paddy. For God's sake, can't you understand?'

She thrust the paper into his hand. 'I've changed my mind about going to the police and you can stop worrying. You're not the same man, darling, so forget the past and the things you were forced to do. I love you, Boris, and Orel is a much nicer name than Dubassof.'

Chapter Twelve

'Of course you'll never be able to forget the past, Boris, but think of the future, as well.' It was just after a quarter to five and they were waiting for Grant in the Landon Arms Hotel. 'You were forced to work for those people and they made you do some horrible things. But you hated the job and were given the chance to get away, so don't torture yourself too much.' Ruth poured out more tea.

'The man called Dubassof was killed when the plane crashed and here's to Boris Orel.'

'Here's to us, darling.' Boris raised his cup. 'And let's hope that Dubassof really is dead and can't return to life. They tried to turn me into a monster and I only pray that the surgery was not perma-nent.' He winced as he looked at the bruise on Ruth's jaw.

'George once said that even someone like Alban could be changed into a decent human being, so perhaps the same applies to me.' A man at the next table was reading a newspaper and Boris saw that the whole centre pages were devoted to the Hangman murders.

'Whatever happens, I want you to know how grateful I will always be to you, Ruth.' He looked away from the bruise and smiled with genuine happiness. And not merely because the threat of returning to Russia had been lifted. He felt clean and at peace with the world for the first time in years because there was one person who trusted him. His story must have revolted Ruth, but she had known how much he had loathed his work and that its memories would haunt him till he died. She had not drawn away as Shura had done, but held out the page from the jotting pad as a gesture of trust and let him take her in his arms. To Ruth, at least, he was not a pariah, and life was wonderful.

'I like you so very, very much, my dear. In fact, I think I love you, Ruth.' He leaned forward and kissed her on the mouth.

'I think I feel the same, Boris, but don't let's show it in here.' The restaurant was an ultra-respectable establishment catering for Castle Landon's elite, and this time she did draw away from him. An elderly waitress hovering near by was looking at them with a shocked expression and two ladies at a window table had raised their eyebrows scornfully.

'And no more worries about Ernest Grant, either, I told him that I know all about you and if he ever mentioned your past, I'd give the police evidence that might prove his lady-love a murderess. You're safe darling, completely safe and . . . Boris, have I been too clever?' Ruth was suddenly troubled and she clasped his hand. 'What about his conscience and self-respect? When Grant's had time to think things over, will he still want the woman? If she killed Eric just to keep out of his way, won't he start to hate her? If so, he might inform on you out of spite.'

'His conscience wouldn't trouble him over Paulson's death, and he already knows that she is desperate to avoid him. If she rejects him to his face he might go round the bend as George considers probable, but we'll have to worry about that when the time comes.' Boris smiled around the room. He felt too happy to really worry about anything. On a dais to their right a string quartet was rendering excerpts from *Iolanthe* with obvious boredom but it seemed the most beautiful music he had ever heard. Ruth trusted him, Ernest Grant must keep his word and the future was assured.

'But what about your own conscience? You said that you had a debt of loyalty to Eric Paulson and to protect me you're going to let his killer get away with it.'

'Like hell I am, Boris. We're handing Miss Reilly over to Deadly Earnest, remember, and I'm quite sure that a few years in prison would be a mild punishment compared to his attentions. I never imagined I could catch a person's aura just from a voice on the telephone, but I got Grant's all right, and I'm sure he's even more unpleasant than you told me.' Ruth sipped her tea thoughtfully. 'When I said to him we'd located the woman he sounded almost boyishly excited for a moment and then became so bloody arrogant that I blurted out her address almost without knowing what I did.

'Then, when I told him about the telephone number on her pad, he broke off and didn't speak for a long time. I thought we'd been disconnected, but when I repeated his name he told me to shut up and keep quiet because he wanted to concentrate. After that it was like listening to a different person and his voice was still domineering but quite without emotion; chilling is the only way I can describe it.

' "Very well, madam", he said. "In view of this information I shall not go directly to the kennels, but meet you and Orel at the Landon Arms Hotel at five o'clock precisely. I will bring you your cheque as promised and also a certain document essential to Mr Orel's peace of mind. If that telephone number is genuine, my hold over him is cancelled out by it and Orel has nothing more to worry about from me. In return I shall expect the seal of secrecy from both of you. Is that understood? Good, then I shall look forward to seeing you at five." He showed absolutely no emotion at all. I felt I was talking to a computer instead of a human being. Yes, you're right, Boris. He didn't seem to care about the possibility that Miss Reilly is probably a murderess. But if he's so obsessed about the woman, why wait till five to meet us? He could have got here hours ago.'

'No, he couldn't. It's common knowledge that Grant has had

a phobia about driving on the open road since his wife's accident. Any speed of more than thirty miles an hour terrifies him.' Boris was still smiling down at their hands clasped together on the table. 'He has obviously taken the afternoon train, but I wonder why he didn't arrange to meet us at the Station Hotel, or on the platform.'

'For the simple reason that I prefer to spend my money where I can get some of it back, Orel.' Like many big men Sir Ernest could move almost silently and they looked up to see him standing above them.

'I own shares in this hotel, so let's have some service.' Grant snapped his fingers at the waitress, laid a spray of orchids on the table and sat down. Though he might have appeared unemotional on the phone, he certainly wasn't now. His face was wreathed in smiles and he made them think of a boy starting out on his holidays.

'You consider that Paddy first tried to bribe your employer and then murdered him when she realized that she couldn't raise the money. And all to escape from my attentions.' Sir Ernest nibbled at a morsel of Dundee cake and washed it down with coffee. 'Not a very complimentary theory, Mrs Renton, but the telephone number suggests that it is the correct one. Yes, I'm afraid I can see Paddy killing Paulson if she thought he was about to lead me to her. She was frightened of me – desperately frightened, and I don't blame her in the slightest. Such a determined girl too, she was. The only person who ever stood up to me for long; maybe that's why I was attracted to her. We are two of a kind and I always thought that we might be distantly related. I never went into it fully, but there seemed to be ties of blood through the female lines.'

'The fact that the woman is probably a murderess doesn't worry you, Sir Ernest?' Ruth watched his face as he considered the question. At practically every other sentence the old man's manner kept changing. One moment he would appear civil and almost friendly, seconds later the cold arrogance she had experienced on the phone would return, and at times he seemed nervous and apprehensive.

'It saddens more than worries me, Mrs Renton. If Paddy did kill Paulson, it was my doing. I turned her into a murderess, and I have

another sin to ask her to forgive.' Apprehension was completely to
the fore now, and Boris and Ruth knew that he was both longing
for the meeting and desperately worried about the reception he
would get. They had imagined that he would have hurried them
out of the hotel as soon as he arrived, but twenty minutes had
passed and he still sipped at his cold coffee and now and again
glanced up at the restaurant clock.

'The possibility encourages me, too, however.' Grant's lips
curved into a bleak smile and he stared at the orchids. 'Paddy has to
learn to love me. I must have time to show her that the past is over
and I am quite different from the man who treated her so badly.
With that telephone number to connect her with the murder, she
won't dare to run away from me again. May I see the page that was
torn from the jotting pad, Orel?

'No, of course not.' He nodded as Boris shook his head. 'You
won't part company with that, my boy, because it negates my
hold over you. You can destroy Paddy just as I can destroy you, so
neither of us can raise a finger against the other.' He took another
morsel of cake and his voice became friendly.

'Strange how fate works things out, Mrs Renton. One day, I
notice Orel's picture in the back number of a trade journal and I
am surprised to see that he is listed under another name. I happen
to have a friend attached to the Russian embassy who drinks more
than he should and talks rather carelessly. From him I learn that
Orel, as he calls himself, was a member of the secret police whom
the Soviet authorities would summon home if they knew he was
alive. I also discover that he has a wife and a young daughter. Orel
is my man and must do exactly what I tell him.' He finished the
dregs of his coffee and beckoned for the waitress to bring the
bill.

'Then fate gets to work again. Almost at the exact moment that
he did what I ordered and found Paddy, you spot a damning piece
of evidence against her, Orel's plight appeals to your emotions,
and he and I are equals.'

Grant signed the bill and then tapped his breast pocket. 'As I
promised I have brought your cheque with me, Mrs Renton, and
also the letter from the bank which concerns you, Orel. If you

are telling the truth you have nothing to worry about. But don't think that I am not prepared for possible treachery. That you may not have found Paddy at all, and hope to silence me when I am on my own with the evidence in my pocket. I know that you once considered killing me, Orel, but I'd advise you not to try today.' He stood up and eased back his jacket to show a shoulder holster and the butt of a revolver. 'I am an old man and I've had a stroke, but I was once a very good shot and I can still move quite quickly. Very well. I think we understand each other, so let's get started.'

He picked up the orchids and led the way across the room, nodding coldly to the head waitress who hurried to open the door for them. His presence at the Landon Arms had been noted and the manager was stationed in the hall with his senior minions spread out behind him. Grant favoured them with another cheerless inclination of his head and moved on towards the rear exit leading to the car park. He walked very slowly, his feet dragging on the carpet and Ruth could sense his nervousness in every footstep. Even though he had the knowledge that might brand Miss Reilly a murderess, he was obviously terrified that she would reject him again. Remembering those small, sharp eyes set deep behind the thick makeup, she imagined that the old man might have more than rejection to worry about. If the woman had killed Eric Paulson to be free of Ernest Grant, would she hesitate to do the same to Paulson's employer?

'Please drive more slowly, Orel. I've waited a long time for this meeting, but there is no need to break our necks.' The Castle Landon rush hour was at its height, the traffic was crawling, but for the second time Sir Ernest growled at him to reduce speed. Through the driving mirror Boris could see that Grant was staring fixedly towards the windscreen while his right hand clutched the armrest to steady himself.

It was Friday night, many of the shops were still open, but there were long queues at the bus stops and the pavements were crowded with office workers on their way home or making for the public houses and a quick one for the road. An ordinary, commonplace scene, but the atmosphere inside the car was strained to breaking point and Boris had begun to share Grant's tension.

What would the meeting be like, he wondered? How would Miss Reilly react when she opened the door and saw the man she had avoided for more than thirty years standing before her? Would she storm at him and scream out her loathing as she had done in the restaurant, or break down and plead with him to leave her alone? Boris fancied that the first reaction was most likely. Somehow he couldn't imagine Paddy Reilly pleading.

THE NECKTIE MURDERS . . . HANGMAN STILL AT LARGE . . . DANEVILLE A CITY OF TERROR. A line of newspaper placards slid by as they turned a corner and began to climb the long slope up from the town centre, and Boris considered how he had once felt that he and Alban had much in common; two evil men running away from their crimes. Now that had been proved an illusion. Harry Alban was an automaton who would go on killing till he was caught because he was controlled by mania, but he himself had been redeemed by Ruth's pardon. Her love and trust had not merely negated Grant's hold over him, she had wiped out the past, the slate was clean and he could start his life again. Soon he would take the letter that Sir Ernest had brought from the bank, snap on his lighter and watch the evidence flare to nothing.

Very, very soon. They were out of the city, shops and offices had given way to suburban houses and the street lights were coming on, though it was still twilight and the rim of the sun clung to the Pennine hills. There was the lay-by where he had made his confession to Ruth. There was the roundabout where she had started to tell him about the telephone number. There, at last, were the gates with the wrought-iron sign 'Riverview Kennels' above them. Ernest Grant tapped his shoulder and told him to stop some twenty yards away from the bungalow.

'You haven't deceived me, then. This really is journey's end, so let's hope that there is a lovers' meeting to go with it.' Grant attempted to speak lightly, but the tic was trembling beneath his cheek and his face shone damp and pallid in the fading light. 'You're a good chap, Orel, and I'll make you a promise here and now. Whatever sort of reception I get from Paddy, you'll find that you've earned more than safety for what you've done for me. I'm a man of my word and Bill Tyrel's job will be yours on the day he retires. I hope those brutes are securely locked up. I've never liked animals and I never will.'

Their arrival had set up a chorus of barks and in the nearest run a big sheepdog seemed beside itself with rage and was bounding against the wire with teeth bared and hackles staring.

'You two had better stay in the car and wait for me.' Sir Ernest's whole body must have been pouring with nervous sweat and they could smell it acrid and pungent against the scent of the orchids.

'Here goes then. Wish me luck if you feel like it.' He climbed out of the car and started to walk down the drive with the spray of flowers clutched in his hand. The curtains of the bungalow were drawn, but there was a light in the porch and as he approached it they saw that his head was bent forward and he was planting his feet very carefully as if fearing a fall.

'He is ill.' The old man had disappeared into the porch, and Ruth laid her hand on Boris's knee. 'Really mentally unbalanced, as his son told you. Those constant changes of manner, the way he kept asking you to drive more slowly, the sweat and the tic on his face. Did you notice that tic, darling?'

'I noticed everything, Ruth. He is a very sick man indeed.' Boris's elation was being replaced by anxiety and he started to open his door. 'And George also believes that he might go completely round the bend if he meets that woman face to face. I think I'd better go and see what . . .'

Boris had been opening the door quite casually, but now he flung it back and hurled himself forward along the drive. The sound he had heard had affected the dogs, too, the barking had risen to a crazed crescendo and their bodies were thudding against the pens as they struggled to break loose. His feet pounded the gravel like pistons, but another shot rang out before he was half-way to the bungalow, and he smelled the tang of cordite as he stumbled up into the porch.

'Stop it, you maniac. Stop it, I say.' The door was open and its lock lay on the floor torn away by the bullets. In the hall beyond he could see that Sir Ernest had finally been reunited with his lost love.

'Let go of her.' Grant was kneeling over the woman and his

hands encircled her neck as if he were throttling the life out of her.
Boris grasped his shoulders, started to drag him away and then
released his grip and drew back.

Sir Ernest Grant was not trying to strangle Paddy Reilly. There
was no need for him to strangle her, because she was dead already.
Ernest Grant was merely loosening a necktie which someone had
left knotted around her throat.

'That's better, isn't it, Paddy? You must be more comfortable
now, so please wake up and look at me.' Ernest Grant had removed
the gaudy tie of blue and yellow polka dots and he cradled the
dead body in his arms. In life, Miss Reilly's face had been small and
compact and her eyes deep-set beneath her forehead. But now the
features were bloated, the eyes bulged from their sockets, and the
skin was dark under the make-up to give her an almost Negroid
appearance.

'Come on, darling, wake up and look at me. It's Ernest, Paddy
and everything's all right at last. We're together again and I've
come to take you home.'

'It's no good. Sir Ernest. Miss Reilly is dead.' Ruth had finished
telephoning the police; the squad cars were on their way, and she
crossed over to him. 'I know that you've had a most terrible shock,
but do try to pull yourself together. She's gone and you must
accept that.'

'Gone – dead, you mean?' Apart from his lips, the old man's face
was as rigid as a graven image and when Ruth laid her hand on his
shoulder she could feel the muscles knotted beneath her touch.
'No, that's not possible, Mrs Renton. Paddy's not dead, she's just
sleeping. She couldn't die before I'd had a chance to talk to her –
before she'd forgiven me. Not when I've been looking for her for
so long.' He nodded his head with complete conviction.

'God wouldn't play a joke on me like that; not on me, surely? He
wouldn't order me to find Paddy and then lead me to her corpse.'
The words stopped and a sound that was part howl, part sob, and
completely animal in its intensity burst from his lips. From outside
a dog bayed in answer.

'No, you're not dead, my darling. You're asleep, Paddy, and I want you to wake up.' When his speech returned it was angry and frustrated and he raised his hand and slapped the lifeless face across the cheek. 'I said wake up, Paddy.'

'Please stop that, sir.' Boris had come back into the room and he caught Grant's arm as he raised it for another blow. 'The woman is dead, she has been murdered, and you must accept that, however much it hurts you.' He helped Ruth to pull him away from the body and lead him to a chair. 'You got through to the police, darling? Good. Whoever killed her came in and also left by the back. The door was ajar and the path outside is muddy. There are two lines of male footprints across the kitchen floor, but the mud has dried, so he'd been gone for some time and there's no point in my trying to follow him.' Boris frowned at the revolver which he had taken from Grant's pocket and put it down on the hall table.

'You mean it's true, really true? You're not lying to me, Orel?' Grant was struggling to return to the woman's body. The dotted necktie flanked her right cheek, and the orchids lay beside her left. Their creamy blooms contrasted horribly with the mottled flesh, and they made Boris think of details from some surrealist painting. Till recently he had hated Ernest Grant passionately, but now he felt nothing except pity towards him.

'But why – why should anybody do this to me? I wanted to find her so desperately, to look after her and win her love again. And all I get is that.' Grant's muscles relaxed, but his eyes remained fixed on the eyes of the corpse. 'I looked through the fanlight after I got no reply from the bell, and I saw her lying there. I thought she was ill, so I broke the lock and went to help her.'

'Yes that's what I thought, darling.' He had been talking to Boris and Ruth, but once again his body stiffened and he tried to struggle forward from the chair. 'I imagined you'd had a stroke like me, Paddy, and had fallen down. We were always two of a kind, weren't we, and neither of us is young. It shook me up to see you look so old, my dear. But not dead, I never thought that you might be dead.' Another howl of anguish echoed around the room. 'And the devil who killed you imagines that he'll get away with a short spell in prison if they catch him. Thirty years they give one for robbing a mail train, but life sentence for murder works out at about nine and a half. He'll be wrong, though, very wrong indeed, Paddy. I've got a good boy, you see. My Mr Orel is very clever at tracing people and he'll find the beast that's responsible. He'll run him down and he'll kill him very slowly and very painfully.' He twisted his hands together and then looked up at Boris.

'It's all right, Orel, I'm in control of myself, so you needn't hang on to me any more.' His face was calm for a moment and Boris and Ruth obeyed him. 'All the same you are going to find the murderer. We won't get involved with the police either, but simply tell them that we came here because I wanted to buy a dog. I don't want to waste time answering endless questions and that's going to be our story. You'll do it for me, won't you, my boy? You'll find Paddy's murderer, if anybody can.' He broke off and his right hand shot out.

'Unless, of course, we don't have to look for the murderer any farther than this room.' Grant had moved very quickly and almost before Boris knew it the revolver was pointing at his chest. 'Stand back, both of you and tell me the truth. Did you kill Paddy, Orel?'

'Don't be a fool, Sir Ernest.' The gun was shaking in his hand, the tic was racking his face again, and Boris braced himself to spring. 'You really must be crazy to think that. Why should I want to kill the woman?'

'Revenge, Comrade Orel. I put the squeeze on you, I made you sweat blood, so maybe you thought you'd pay me back. Yes, an ex-M.V.D. official might think it funny to present me with a dead body.' The muzzle of the revolver was jerking from side to side and Grant pulled back his hand to steady it against his chest. As he did so, he felt the bulge in his pocket and frowned.

'No, I'm not talking sense, am I? You may hate me, but you wouldn't have dared to injure Paddy; not when I have the means to ruin you . . . to send you back to Russia.' He snapped on the safety catch and replaced the pistol on the table.

'Sorry, Orel. My apologies to you as well, Mrs Renton. I hope you'll both forget that exhibition. Maybe I should see a psychiatrist as George keeps advising. The fact is that I'm beginning to develop a kind of persecution complex. First Madge's accident, then my stroke and my craving to see Paddy; now this.' The tic had left Grant's face and he spoke and looked perfectly normal as he glanced towards the doorway. The dogs had started to bark again and headlights were turning in from the main road.

'Now, remember our story. I've been lonely since my wife died and I thought a dog would be company. I sent you here to select one for me, because I was too busy to come myself.' He watched the approaching lights and his voice was full of his usual authority. 'You made a choice, but I changed my mind and felt I'd better come and look the animal over before taking delivery. None of us had ever set eyes on Paddy before today. Is that clear?'

'Quite clear, but I want that letter and Mrs Renton's cheque now, Sir Ernest: also a promise that you'll keep your word.' Boris held out his hand, Grant reached in his pocket, but they were both too late. Tyres skidded to a halt on the gravel, doors slammed and the police came pouring into the hall.

Chapter Thirteen

'Perfectly true, Inspector Palmer. No one denies that it is an odd coincidence that Mr Orel and Mrs Renton should have discovered the bodies of two murder victims within just over thirty hours of each other.' Commander Norman Trant of Scotland Yard was young for his high rank and had a pleasant boyish face which hid an acid tongue and an extremely poor opinion of his provincial colleagues.

'But, as we all know, coincidences do happen, gentlemen.' He smiled blandly at his audience. Colonel Standish, the chief constable of Northmoorland, an elderly, ill-tempered and very worried man, six senior officers from the Daneville and Castle Landon forces, and the head warder of Seamont prison. Because the crimes attributed to Alban had taken place in the two cities, Trant had been sent to co-ordinate operations.

'They happen all too frequently, Commander.' A Castle Landon superintendent spoke from a corner seat of the conference room. The failure to capture the Hangman and their future plans had been discussed with some acrimony and tempers were frayed. 'But

I still consider that Alban may have nothing to do with Miss Anderson's murder. She appears to be a bit of a mystery woman, and
little is known about her before she settled in this city five years
ago. Isn't it possible that some person who wanted her out of the
way may have regarded the two earlier murders as a godsend and
imitated Alban's methods?'

'It's possible, Superintendent. In fact I've read the detective story
in which the ruse occurs.' Trant stifled a yawn ostentatiously.
'Highly unlikely, though, and in my opinion there is not the slightest doubt that Alban is responsible for all three murders.'

'Which means that he slipped through the cordons because of
idleness and inefficiency.' The chief constable scowled at Palmer
who headed the Daneville contingent. 'If you people had been dili-
gent enough to search every vehicle leaving the area that maniac
would be safely behind bars. As it is, he got past you, he has killed
again and will have probably moved on to another town. At any
moment a fourth body may be reported and we're sitting on our
backsides discussing Orel, the Renton woman and Sir Ernest
Grant. A complete waste of time, gentlemen. They went to the
kennels to buy a dog and that's all there is to it.'

'Then why should Grant have had a gun with him, sir?' Like the
chief constable, the superintendent was old and irascible. 'Surely
that smells to heaven?'

'The woman was strangled, not shot, Super, and Sir Ernest had
a licence for the revolver,' Standish flared back at him. 'He bought
it in 1957 after being threatened by a workman whom he sacked
and he'd got into the habit of carrying the thing about with him.
It's quite natural that he should break the lock when he saw the
woman's body on the floor, and we can rule him out as a murder
suspect.'

'I bow to your years and experience, sir, but we can rule nothing
out till the killer is sentenced.' Trant had stressed the chief constable's age with a sneer. 'At the same time, it is most unlikely that
there can be any connection except coincidence between the
Paulson and Anderson murders. Mrs Renton was out of the
country when Paulson was killed, and neither she nor Orel could
have murdered Miss Anderson. The body temperature makes it

clear that the woman was strangled between four and five o'clock and during that time they were drinking tea in the Landon Arms Hotel.' Trant consulted his notes and stood up.

'Their statements tally, and unless we can find a motive, we must accept them. Sir Ernest sends Orel to find him a dog and Mrs Renton goes along for the ride, as one says.' The commander gave an arch smile that drew no response. 'Orel telephones Grant to say that he has found a suitable animal, but Grant decides that he'd better look at it himself before taking delivery. They meet at the hotel and that's that. The story holds water and Bob is a very close relative indeed.' He ignored the colonel's snort of annoyance at his flippancy and nodded towards two photographs of Alban displayed on the wall.

'Everything points to that loony, unless you think we should consider the kennelmaid, Rose Crichton. She arrived home at four fifteen, half an hour earlier than usual, and told her mother that Miss Anderson had threatened her with bodily violence and she was packing up the job. Any takers for Rose as a suspect, gentlemen, she's a big powerful girl?' He watched them shake their heads and moved over to the photographs.

'Yes, this must be the blighter we want, all right. Harry Alban committed all three murders and he'll kill again if we don't pull him in soon.' He consulted his watch and frowned. 'That fellow, Gompals, from the Home Office is late and I hope nothing's held him up. I don't usually value the opinions of outside experts, but we are out of our depth and he might have an idea or two. If only there was something distinctive about Alban's appearance; a scar, or a limp, or vivid red hair. Apart from his size he looks so damned commonplace. Tomorrow afternoon there'll be thousands of men resembling him yelling their heads off at every football match in the country.' Trant nodded towards the nondescript features of the strangler.

'If the women were tarts or girls he'd picked up in pubs, or cafés, or dance halls we might get him by using policewomen as decoys. But his victims are all so ordinary and quite unknown to him. Middle-aged women whom he spotted in the street, followed and murdered when the coast was clear. That is almost certainly what happened in the case of Miss Anderson. She visited a local grocer's shop shortly before four and said she was going straight back to the kennels. The bastard must have come across her on her way home. Sorry, I didn't catch that, Colonel.' He turned from the photographs as the chief constable repeated his question. 'Yes, though Alban did not rob any of his victims, it is possible that he may have money to support himself for a few days. You will remember those dud fifty-pence pieces which were going the rounds during the spring, gentlemen? Well, though we never managed to prove it, there is evidence to suggest that they may have been produced during metalwork classes at Seamont prison.'

'Good grief.' Colonel Standish thumped his chair arm and glowered at the prison officer. 'Your security arrangements leave much to be desired, Mr Bates. Not only are homicidal maniacs allowed to walk away from Seamont as free as air, but coiners are encouraged to ply their trade. Still, that's only to be expected, I suppose. The happiness of your poor, lost sheep must always come first.'

'That is an unfair remark, sir, and I must point out that I personally protested when Harry Alban was allowed outside privileges. It was the governor, and . . .' The warder started to defend himself, but at that moment the door burst open and they all turned to see an enormously stout man enter the room.

'Gompals . . . Dr Barry Gompals.' The man bowed and announced his name with a deal of pride. Though about sixty years old he was dressed in the height of teenage fashion with a velveteen jacket and striped linen trousers. A fringe of dyed, ginger locks hung over his collar, he had a flowing moustache of the same shade and a long, fat cigar jutted from his lips.

'Sorry to have kept you waiting, but the bloody train was late.' He hurried forward to the dais and laid his briefcase on the table.

'Now, let me state my qualifications, gentlemen. I am a doctor of medicine, a member of the British Institute of Morbid Psychology, an honorary fellow of the universities of Oxford, Columbia and . . .' He was obviously enjoying the introduction, but Trant cut him short.

'We know your professional standing, Dr Gompals, so may we get down to business?'

'As you wish, Mr Trant, but I must make it clear that I am a senior Home Office adviser and have been sent to instruct you.' The fat man opened his briefcase with a flourish and sat down.

'Harry Alban – the Mad Hangman, as he is called. A simple-minded maniac, who since his escape has been running rings round you and murdered two women; possibly three. I have only just been informed about the last killing, but the pattern appears to be the same and it must be Alban's work.' He drew a stack of notes and photographs from the case and arranged them neatly before him.

'Though the dossier did not reach me till yesterday and I have never interviewed Alban, I have read the report of Cox, the resident psychiatrist at Seamont, with interest and surprise. He states that Alban was responding to treatment; hence the outside privileges which were given to him. But he also admits that Alban had complained of night terrors during the last few months. In my considered opinion Dr Cox is an irresponsible fool and guilty of gross professional negligence. I see that you agree with me, gentlemen.'

He waited for the murmurs of approval to die down. 'Alban may have been responding to treatment; he was a docile and co-operative prisoner who seemed eager to please everyone, but to me those nightmares would have been a clear warning that his mania had merely been driven underground and was building up again. You might compare it to a haystack that has not been properly dried out. The surface is damp and cold, but inside heat is developing and very soon combustion is bound to take place. Excuse that rather clumsy simile, but as you are all laymen, I must state the facts as simply as possible. Now, have you a photograph of this Miss . . . Miss Anderson I can look at?'

Commander Trant produced one and Gompals examined it with a knowing smile.

'Gentlemen, my theory is fitting together very nicely, and your troubles may soon be over. All we have to do is to concentrate on the victims and forget their murderer. Pass these around for me, will you?' He handed Trant five of the photographs he had brought with him but left one on the desk. 'Alban's victims, gentlemen.

Women with a marked physical resemblance to one another: slightly built, fair-haired, and with rather small and piercing eyes. Those killed in London before his arrest ten years ago ranged in age from forty-one to forty-six. The recent victims, if we include Miss Anderson were fifty-two, fifty-six and fifty-nine.' His pudgy hand dipped into the case again and he produced a child's drawing pad, shaking his head petulantly before passing it to Trant.

'This was found in Alban's cell after the escape and you might call it a pin-up album. Pictures of women cut from newspapers and magazines and pasted in. You will recognize a few public figures in the collection. There is an actress, an M.P. and a novelist, but most of them are unknown to me.'

'The resemblances are quite uncanny.' Trant was turning the pages. 'All these women are of the same physical type. Some of them might almost be related.'

'They are not merely related, gentlemen. They happen to be the same woman and Alban is killing her over and over again.' The doctor paused impressively and puffed at his cigar.

'The age difference between his earlier victims and the three recent ones is most significant in my opinion. Harry Alban is growing older, so the woman he must destroy ages as well. All we have to do is to find her original and your problems are solved. No interruptions till I have discussed motivation, please.' Standish had attempted to ask a question, but Gompals thumped the desk for silence. 'Harry Alban was abandoned in a railway carriage when he was about six years old. He was feeble-minded, did not appear to remember his own surname, and refused to talk about his past. He was given the name Alban because St Albans was the destination of the train.

'But though a slow-witted child, he had a craving for love, and attempted to obtain it from the orphanage matron, a Mrs Hilda Oliver. From the day he was put in her charge Harry Alban tried to attach himself to Mrs Oliver and followed her about like a dog. The relationship was tragic in the extreme and it accounts for everything.

'Mrs Oliver is alive and has been traced. I have spoken to her and she was both frank and helpful. Though she felt sorry for

Alban he was not an attractive child and his physical presence repelled her. That was natural because he was an air-swallower, he wet his bed every night and was unclean in his person generally. However much Mrs Oliver might pity him, she resented his attentions and on a few occasions she actually struck out at him. Usually the boy merely wept or cringed away, but at the end he responded violently.' Barry Gompals handed Trant the last photograph.

'When he was approaching puberty, Alban could not accept rejection any more and love turned to hatred. Mrs Oliver pushed him away once too often and he went berserk and tried to strangle her. No, not with a tie. He used his hands for the simple reason that there was no tie available. The children always wore jerseys or open-necked shirts and resented the fact. Because of the attack he was transferred to another home and some months later Mrs Oliver and her husband emigrated to Canada. They returned to this country only last year.'

'This is Mrs Oliver?' Trant had almost snatched the photograph from him. 'The same physical type and age group as the others all right. And you believe that in his mind that maniac is killing this one woman over and over again, Dr Gompals? That ten years after leaving the orphanage he saw a woman who reminded him of her and something snapped. All because she rejected him when he was a child?'

'I believe it's possible, Commander. The Jesuits say, "Give us a child when he is seven and he is ours for the rest of his natural life", and we know that love and hate are very often related. It is also true that if a craving is indulged, but not fully satisfied, the desire becomes even more obsessive.

'Yes, I believe that Mrs Oliver is Harry's constant victim, that he is looking for her all the time and she'd have been dead long ago if she hadn't gone abroad where he couldn't find her.'

'Thank you, Doctor.' Trant beamed at the photograph. 'So, if you're right, we've got him. Have Mrs Oliver up here, make her appeal to Alban in the press and on the radio and television and say that her feelings have changed and she wants to meet him again.' He snapped his fingers and beamed at his fellow officers, though he felt a brief twinge of pity as he thought of the little subnormal boy who had craved for love and been rejected. All the same, he was a policeman whose duty it was to protect the public and compassion for a killer was inappropriate. 'If the doctor is right and Alban is all that crazy, we've got him, gentlemen. He may fear arrest, but he won't be able to control himself. When Matron appeals to the child in her charge, the Hangman is bound to come running.'

Chapter Fourteen

'You shouldn't have come in today, sir. Not after the terrible shock you had yesterday.' Michael Byrne had been passing the door of George's office which was open and seen the old man standing in the centre of the floor and staring around him as though he hardly knew where he was.

'When I rang the house early this morning they told me that the doctor had ordered you to stay in bed and rest.' Byrne was a short, stockily built Dubliner who had modelled his public image on the stage Irishman and his manner varied between deep gloom for the sufferings of the Celts and saloon-bar heartiness: 'Have another jar and I'll tell you how Pat and Fergus beat up the Murphy gang at the Loutstown races.' Beneath these public images lay an astute business brain and it was sometimes said in the firm, 'Shake hands with your Uncle Mike, me bhoy, and you'll find that his free hand's lifted your wallet.' At the moment gloom was well to the fore. He had been Sir Ernest's personal assistant for five years and Grant was the only human being for whom he felt a shred of affection.

'The doctor knows nothing, Mike, and I've had more than a shock. As you must have guessed by now, the woman whose body we found was Paddy Reilly.' Grant had told Byrne about his search for Miss Reilly, because the man was his protégé, he relied on his gratitude and trusted him completely. He had good reason to do so. When they first met the Irishman had been in serious financial difficulties, but Sir Ernest had recognized his ability and paid off a large number of irate creditors. Without that help Michael Byrne would still be serving a sentence for fraud, and in return Grant had his unswerving loyalty.

'If my doctor had known about our relationship and what Paddy means to me, I'd be too full of dope to move.' He shook his head at the collection of railway photographs. 'I hoped to talk to George, Michael. I wanted to confide in him and tell him that he was right about Paddy all the time.'

'But George never comes into the office on Saturday mornings, sir. Didn't you know that?' Byrne watched him with deep concern. Not only was Grant's face pinched, but his whole body looked frail and shrunken. He must have been lying down in his usually immaculate suit and it hung about him in folds and made Byrne think of him as a pupa that had withered in its cocoon.

'He told me some time ago, Michael, but I'd forgotten, and the desk had to remind me just now. Every Friday evening George packs up and goes to work on his blasted railway in North Wales.' He shook his head at the photograph of a Bryncir 0-4-0 tank locomotive. 'I would have thought that just for once – just for today of all days he might have put off the expedition. He was very upset when I told him that Orel had located Paddy and I was going to Castle Landon to see her, but when George heard that she was dead he might have stuck by me.'

'But he couldn't have known Miss Reilly was dead, sir. He always sets out at five o'clock sharp and I don't suppose he reads the paper when he's busy with his hobby.' Byrne frowned at an aerial view of the Bryncir railway. Though George could not have heard about the murder he felt waves of bitterness that he was not on hand to comfort his father.

'No, of course, he doesn't know and thanks for reminding me. I'm always misjudging poor old George, it seems. When I first told him that I was going to try and find Paddy, he pleaded with me not to and I imagined that his motives were financial. I suspected that he was frightened that I might cut him out of my will and this tomfoolery must cost him a packet.' Sir Ernest was still studying the photographs. 'Then I thought that it was affection he wanted. After Madge was killed George hoped we'd become real friends and have a proper father-son relationship at last.' He turned away from the wall with a shrug and walked across to the desk.

'But lying in bed this morning, I began to understand that

George has a wisdom I never credited him with. He knew that things could never have worked out for Paddy and me and he wanted to protect us from each other.'

Grant lowered himself into George's chair and cupped his left hand against his forehead. 'George knew that Paddy and I could only hurt each other, and he was right. I started to realize that myself when I knelt down over her poor little body in that bungalow that stank of dogs. I hardly recognized her face at first, Michael, and not because she'd been strangled and the features were so hideously distorted. I just hadn't believed that she'd have altered so much over the years – that my Paddy would have grown old. I've always kept thinking of her as a girl, you see. Crazy, isn't it? When I was in hospital I heard voices and I kept seeing her face. I thought I'd had a vision ordering me to make things up with Paddy. How presumptuous can one get? What I experienced were delusions produced by cerebral damage during the stroke; an "insult to the brain" is what doctors call the condition. But because I believed in them Paddy's dead and I'm responsible.'

'You responsible, sir?' Byrne's Dublin accent was harsh. 'Now, just you stop talking like that, or you really will make yourself ill again. You're naturally shaken up because Miss Reilly's dead, but you had nothing to do with her murder. That escaped madman came across her by chance and you've no reason to reproach yourself.'

'Chance? That power has been working overtime recently. Several hundred people vanish without trace in this country each month, yet by pure strokes of luck both Paulson and Boris Orel were able to locate Paddy. Oh, yes, Michael, Paulson did find Paddy, and there is a strong possibility that she murdered him to escape from me.' Grant's trust in Byrne was so complete that he did not hesitate to tell the truth.

'If that is correct . . . if Paddy's hatred was strong enough to make her commit murder on my account, isn't it logical that Harry Alban might have been an instrument sent to punish us both? You're a lapsed Catholic, Michael, but surely you still believe in divine retribution. That God sometimes employs human agencies to destroy the arrogant. I certainly do, and I'm quite sure that

Paddy would be alive if it wasn't for my presumption and her cruelty.'

'I believe no such nonsense, Sir Ernest, and life's got to go on, so for Christ's sake try and snap out of it.' Byrne's manner changed to a brusque heartiness. 'And by the way, I've got some interesting news for you. Peter Brown was admitted to hospital for a gallstone operation last night, so what about our take-over bid? Twelve shillings was the offer you last decided on.'

'Then twelve shillings it will be.' There was a tiny gleam of interest in Sir Ernest's eyes. 'We both know that the rest of the directors are greedy sheep and my guess is that they'll grab it without a single dissension. Peter is the only real businessman Salinger-Brown have got.' He reached in his pocket and drew out two envelopes. 'Life must go on, as you say, and that reminds me that I've got a couple of debts to settle. Give these to Boris Orel with my compliments, please. One's for him and the other's for the Renton girl.'

'No, on second thoughts I'll hand them over myself.' Byrne had reached out for the envelopes, but he shook his head and replaced them in his pocket. 'I'd trust you with my life, Michael, but not with anybody else's and you're also an inquisitive chap. No one is going to know what Orel was paid for his services. Oh, damn George and his stupid hobby. I did want to talk to him so badly.'

Grant had been smiling faintly, but frowned as he looked at the tiny tape recorder lying on the desk. 'I fiddled with this contraption to steady my nerves and the mechanism seems to be faulty and it came on of its own accord. Just listen.' He pressed the switch and the sounds of a locomotive pounding up an incline reverberated through the loudspeaker.

'How pathetic. A grown man playing with toy trains.' Sir Ernest turned off the set. 'Madge and I were to blame, I suppose. George had a lonely boyhood with only toys to amuse him, and he's never grown out of them. I've done George a terrible injury, and I've got to confide in him. I've got to explain just how it all happened. Now, though you're a good friend, Michael, I'm quite all right, and I want to be left alone for a bit. So push off and do some work on the Salinger-Brown deal. I'll give you a buzz later on and we'll go through the draft together over lunch. See you about one, then.'

He watched the Irishman close the door behind him and then walked back to George's collection of photographs with the tape recorder still clutched in his hand. He looked from one picture to another, trying to understand why his adopted son should find the hobby so fascinating, but failing. What did George see in those small, archaic carriages and outlandish locomotives that might chug impressively over the fells, but were completely inefficient, and would never earn their keep? Why should George prefer them to the vast, modern machines which served Aly's interests? Almost without thinking, Sir Ernest switched on the recorder and listened to wheels grinding over points, pistons thudding, steam roaring through the exhaust valves, and George shouting some incomprehensible order to his fireman.

Then the noise of the train ceased and apart from the whirr of the spools there was a sudden silence. Grant frowned till he remembered that the apparatus had a fault and switched itself on and off at times.

But something was coming through the loudspeaker again. A series of light taps, that could be feet walking quickly along a wooden floor, a pause, the sound of a door opening and closing, a man's voice which he felt he should recognize, but could not place at first. Then the man spoke again, another voice replied to him and the recorder dropped from Grant's hand. He knew who the voices belonged to now . . . he knew what they had been about to say and he leaned against the wall to steady himself. He felt weak with sudden shock, but his face was no longer pale and drawn and bewildered. It was full of anger and as dark as Paddy Reilly's dead face had been.

A few hours after the tape recorder fell from Ernest Grant's hand, another switch had been pressed and another recording echoed around a room. It was pop music, the Vagrants' latest number, 'Fly Me Away There', and the man who was listening smiled and clapped his hands in time to the tune. He had been nervous about turning on the radio, but the three Vagrants, Mack, Mick and Marion were his favourite group and he had almost come to regard them as personal friends.

Fly me away there,
Anywhere away there
Anywhere away from her.

That was the stuff. His hands clapped louder and louder and he joined in the chorus. 'Anywhere – anywhere away from her.'

What had happened? When the song ended an announcer had broken in and was interrupting the programme. That wasn't fair at all. The music had only started a few minutes ago and they had no right to interrupt just when he was enjoying himself so much. In his disappointment he tried to close his mind to what was being said and think of other things till the Vagrants came on again.

'No, no, no, that's not true.' He had been stretched out on his bed, but now he was sitting bolt upright and the words were torn from his lips in gasps. 'She went far away and she'll never come back. Either that or she's dead – dead – dead like the others. You're just telling lies to torture me.'

He tried to force himself to get up and turn off the radio, but his limbs refused to obey him and all at once the glowing dial faded and was replaced by a story-book illustration that had terrified him as a child. Hercules fighting the monster with nine heads which he could not kill because as soon as one head was struck off two more grew in its place. Different heads on one body and their faces were all identical. God, how they frightened him!

'Harry Alban, this is Mrs Oliver talking to you.' A woman's voice had replaced the announcer's, but the man did not hear her. He had thrown himself back on the bed, buried his face in the pillow and thrust his fingers into his ears. He lay like that for a full five minutes, not daring to move till he felt certain that the coast was clear. Then very cautiously he uncovered his ears, heard that the music had been resumed and stood up.

The wardrobe door was open showing the line of neckties hanging from their press and his confidence returned as he walked towards them. However frightened he might be, he was not alone and there was always a temporary escape from the multi-headed Hydra that could never die.

Chapter Fifteen

'Grant may be cruel and without mercy, darling, but you've done what he asked and I don't believe he's spiteful.' Ruth watched Boris restlessly pacing the sitting-room of his flat. 'In any case he must keep his word. He knows that if he raised a finger against you, I'd go straight to the press and the police and make the whole story public.'

'You're talking as though he's mentally normal, Ruth.' Boris crossed to the telephone. 'While Grant's in a rational mood, he'll keep quiet, but his mind's balanced on a knife edge. Remember how he accused us of the murder? If that notion comes back, he'll say to hell with the consequences and contact the Soviet embassy immediately. I must get hold of that letter.'

For the third time that morning Boris dialled Sir Ernest's private number, and while he listened to the ringing tone he pictured the old man lying in bed and brooding over what had happened. Grant's periods of irrationality appeared to be brief and while he was himself there was probably nothing to fear. But if the suspicion that he and Ruth had killed Miss Reilly returned, it might last long enough for him to have the letter posted.

'My name is Orel and I have called before. I know that Sir Ernest is ill, but it is imperative that I speak to him.' The housekeeper had answered, but this time she did not repeat that her employer was still resting and accepting no calls. Half an hour ago Grant had got up and ordered a taxi to take him to the Allied Building.

'I beg your pardon, sir.' The woman was clearly astonished by his question. 'Yes, he was, but I really . . .'

'Thank you.' Boris banged down the phone triumphantly. 'He's at the office, Ruth, and he is wearing the same suit as he did yesterday. With any luck at all, those envelopes will still be on him, so let's go.' He helped her on with her coat and they hurried off to collect their rewards.

It was a pleasant day. A bright autumn morning drifting into afternoon and the centre of Daneville was thronged with Saturday shoppers and here and there they passed groups of men and boys wearing football favours in anticipation of United's home match against Chelsea. The sky was clear and people were smiling again. The Hangman might still be at large, but he had moved away to another town and the citizens of Daneville could relax. Very soon Boris and Ruth might be able to relax with them.

Or could they? Boris kept asking himself. Even when that letter was destroyed, could he ever feel safe? If Grant's suspicions returned, he could write another letter or make a telephone call to the embassy. Only when Sir Ernest died would he feel completely free.

But men die easily and he had been taught a useful trade. Boris thought of Peter Vanin and his other instructors while he nosed the car through the traffic, and he knew that the technical problems were slight. Accidents do happen, strokes recur and old people lose their sense of balance. They fall on staircases and railway platforms and stumble in front of motor vehicles. Just one quick push, Sir Ernest Grant would be dead, and neither Ruth nor anyone else would guess who had killed him.

What are you thinking about? He forced the notion out of his mind as the Allied Building loomed up before him. Boris Dubassof had been a murderer. He had been trained to kill and betray like a conditioned dog that drools at the mouth when the dinner bell is rung. But Dubassof was dead and done with and he was Boris Orel. He couldn't kill anybody; not even Ernest Grant who might ruin him at a whim. All he could do was to destroy that letter and leave the future to fate. Boris parked the car and he and Ruth walked towards the entrance hall.

'Sir Ernest, sir?' Though Aly always maintained a skeleton staff on Saturdays, there was only one receptionist behind the desk; a large imposing man with a fine display of medal ribbons on his uniform jacket whom Boris always thought of as the 'Soviet marshal'. 'I've just taken over from Sergeant Watkins, but I'll check for you, Mr Orel.' He turned to the switchboard to contact Michael Byrne.

'Sir Ernest did come in and apparently he's in Mr George's

office, but there's no good going up, sir. He is not to be disturbed on any account. Not on any account, Mr Orel.' He shouted the last sentence and addressed himself to Byrne again because Boris and Ruth were already hurrying to a lift.

George's room was on the fifteenth floor and Boris's hopes surged as they slid towards it. The letter and Ruth's cheque must still be in Grant's pocket and in a few seconds he would keep his promise and hand them over. Should he refuse they would be taken from him. Boris might not be able to kill but he would have no compunction about using force.

'One moment, Mr Orel.' The office faced the lift shaft, but Michael Byrne was stationed before the door when they stepped out. 'I understand that you didn't hear the message I gave to the desk sergeant. Sir Ernest is not feeling at all well after his tragic experience and does not wish to be disturbed.'

'I know that he's not well, Mr Byrne, and Mrs Renton and I were with him when he found the woman's body. But he will want to see us all right, and it is essential that I talk to him at once.'

'Sorry, but the answer is still no.' Byrne bristled like a watchdog. If Sir Ernest had become wearied of his own company, he wasn't going to be bothered by a nobody like Orel. 'If there is anything I can do, I'd be glad to help you.'

'What you can do is to either step aside or tell Sir Ernest that I am here, Mr Byrne.' Boris resisted the urge to push the Irishman out of his way. 'He has some most important documents to give us.'

'Umhm, he did say that.' Byrne hesitated. The boss, as he always thought of Grant, had mentioned payments for Orel and this Mrs Renton and he had seen the envelopes. They might be important, and though the boss was ill he had better check with him.

'All right, I'll ask him if he wants to see you, but please try not to keep him long.' He turned and opened the door very gently. 'Sorry to interrupt you, Sir Ernest, but . . . Are you there, sir?'

He stood frowning around the room which was empty, though Grant's hat and coat lay on a chair near the window. 'Strange that. I only left him about a quarter of an hour ago.' Byrne crossed over to another door and looked into the secretary's cubicle which was also empty.

'Christ, you don't think that . . . ?' The window was wide open and he rushed towards it and leaned out, obviously fearing that Grant's body would be lying on the pavement below. 'No, of course the boss wouldn't do that. I've got too much ruddy imagination and I am worried about him. The old boy really was in a bad way. He came here to talk to George – to tell him that he'd been wrong to look for the Reilly woman. That he was responsible for her death, because they both had to be punished by some divine force. He even suggested that she had killed the detective to escape from him. All nonsense, of course. I don't think he really knew what he was saying half the time. Hang on a moment.' Byrne's face cleared and he hurried past them into the corridor.

'Don't worry, Boris.' Ruth nodded towards Grant's briefcase and the hat and coat. 'His things are here so he must be somewhere in the building. Probably he's gone to his own room or is having a wash.'

'No, I've looked in the cloakroom and he couldn't have gone back to his own office without my seeing him. Just where the hell has he got to?' Michael Byrne had come back and he snatched the house telephone from the desk.

'Sergeant Abbot, has the boss left the building during the last twenty minutes or so?' His rather prominent eyebrows came up in a bar at the man's reply. 'Look, Sergeant, I don't give a bugger that you've only been on duty for half that time. You know damn well that the movements of all executive staff to and from the head office have to be recorded, so look in the bloody log book and be quick about it. Nothing entered, eh, but he had a call to the transport depot. Put me through to them.' Byrne's anxiety had vanished, but his face was sad while he waited with the receiver at his ear. 'He must have felt really ill, Orel. We had a lunch date, but he can't have remembered it and sent for a car to take him home. Poor old chap, he really is in a bad way. Not like the boss to forget an appointment with me.

'Transport depot? You take your time to answer, don't you? It's Mr Byrne here and I understand that Sir Ernest ordered a car to drive him home a short time ago. What – what's that? But it's just not possible, man. You know perfectly well that he has not driven a car for months.' Anxiety had returned with a rush and Byrne's knuckles were white on the telephone. 'Oh, I see. That settles it, then.' He shook his head as if he could not believe his ears and rattled the phone rest to get back to the sergeant.

'Abbot, I want you to telephone Sir Ernest's residence and tell them to call me the moment he arrives there.' He banged down the instrument and stared at Boris and Ruth.

'Jesus, I was right to be worried. The old boy hasn't gone home; at least it doesn't seem very likely. He ordered his own car, and told 'em to fill up the petrol tank and bring her round to the rear entrance. There's no mistake because the chap I spoke to attended to it himself and saw him drive off. Yes, he has got a phobia about driving, Mrs Renton, and that's what worries me; no, terrifies me is the better word.' Byrne had pulled out a cigarette as Ruth spoke and his hand was shaking so badly that he could hardly bring his lighter to its tip. 'He once told me that he suspected his wife might have killed herself and piled-up her car deliberately. Since her death he's never touched a steering wheel till today.

'And this business just now. Saying that he wanted to tell George; confide was the word he used, that he was responsible for the Reilly-Anderson woman's murder. He was rambling, of course, but a guilt complex can be a dangerous thing and his parents were fanatical Calvinists who brought him up strictly. He's been in a bad way since his stroke and after what happened yesterday, I wouldn't put anything past him.' Byrne started to give them a résumé of what Grant had said and then frowned.

'But what the hell am I doing standing here talking when the boss may be in danger!' He grabbed the outside phone, dialled emergency and asked for the police.

'My name is Michael Byrne, officer, and I want to report a possible suicide attempt . . . Grant . . . Sir Ernest Grant . . . driving a black Rover Three Litre, registration number AVK 995H . . . probably heading for the Pennine motorway . . .' He voiced his fears and warnings in jerky, half-formed sentences. 'Lady Grant killed on motorway last May . . . hit a bridge six miles north of the Naeswirth service area . . . please try and stop him, officer . . . please. You want a full statement from me? Yes, naturally, I'll come to the station immediately, but do put an emergency call out.' He let the telephone fall on to the desk and rushed out of the room without another glance at Ruth and Boris.

'Do you believe it's possible, Ruth?' Boris tried to imagine Ernest Grant bent over the steering wheel of a car with the nervous tic trembling below his cheek and his eyes wide open with horror as he approached the place where his wife had died. He tried to form a picture of Grant's hand swinging the wheel over while the bridge came hurtling towards him and his eyes closing just before the moment of impact. But somehow the images refused to appear. Grant was racked with remorse for his wife's death and the way he had treated Paddy Reilly in the past. He might have developed an insane illusion that he was also responsible for Miss Reilly's murder, and he was a very ruthless man. But though Sir Ernest might be capable of many things, Boris did not consider that suicide was one of them.

'No, Boris, Grant would never kill himself. He has a guilt complex and was brought up as a Calvinist. Most probably he believes in hell fire and that suicide is an unforgivable sin.' Ruth was looking at George's photographs and the other illustrations on the wall.

'He came to the office to talk to George and he had his car filled up with petrol, which suggests a long journey. You told me that George spends his weekends in North Wales, so surely that is where he's gone? He wants to talk to George and confide in him. Yes, confide was what he said to Byrne and the word means the same thing as confess.'

'Confess to what?' Byrne had left the telephone lying on the desk and Boris replaced it in its rest. 'George knows all about his search for the woman.'

'But George may not know that his father found her, Boris; found her body, that is. If he was at all fond of the old man he'd hardly have gone off and left him in the lurch. He doesn't know the end of the story, and neither do we know the middle. Yes, the middle, darling. The events that happened between the time I telephoned Grant and he met us in the hotel. You see I'm starting to wonder if he wasn't raving when he told Byrne that he was responsible for her death.' Ruth's back was still towards Boris and she ran a finger along a coloured contour map, tracing the route of the Port Olwyn and Bryncir Railway.

'I suppose Harry Alban must have strangled those women in Daneville, but isn't it possible and quite likely that Grant is a good actor and he murdered Miss Reilly himself?'

'I've been trained to have a suspicious mind, Ruth, but this is too much to swallow.' Boris had been listening to her in silence but now he broke in. 'It's physically possible, I suppose. Grant appears to have conquered his fears of driving, and he could have taken a car to Castle Landon, and had ample time to kill the woman, garage the car with instructions that it would be called for later, and meet us in the hotel as if he'd come off the afternoon train. Also, a man of his intelligence would obviously have hit on the idea of imitating Alban's method to throw the blame on him.

'Your theory holds water in that sense, and Grant had attacked the woman physically in the past. George also believed that he might do so again if he found her and she refused him out of hand. But I still can't accept that he went near that bungalow on his own. He couldn't have killed her, darling, because he was out of his mind: insane with grief and shock. Hell, you must remember how he behaved.'

'Insane with grief. Maybe that's the correct term, Boris. There is a quotation that says, "Each man kills the thing he loves."' Ruth had turned from the wall and was staring out of the window. The sky was still clear and beyond the town she could see the long, white ribbon of the motorway stretching towards Castle Landon.

'If an unbalanced person did something on impulse and then bitterly regretted it, isn't it possible that guilt might produce a blackout and he would begin to believe that somebody else was responsible?'

'But that's the whole weakness of your theory, Ruth. You're suggesting that after talking to you, Grant changed his mind about the train and decided to take a car and go straight to Miss Reilly. When she refused to have anything to do with him, he lost control and strangled her on impulse. It won't wash, darling, because where did he get hold of the necktie?' Michael Byrne was probably right, Boris thought. Ernest Grant might well be dead by now and his car a shattered wreck beside the motorway. He hoped it was a blazing wreck, too. Grant had mentioned their payments to Byrne and the envelopes must be on him. With Sir Ernest dead and that letter turned into charred fragments his worries were over. All he need think about were the pleasant ways to compensate Ruth for the loss of her five thousand pounds.

'You've completely missed the point, Boris.' She left the window and walked over to him. 'I think Grant decided to kill Miss Reilly while I talked to him on the telephone. When he heard that we had located her, he sounded excited; almost happy, but after I mentioned the probability that she was Eric Paulson's killer, he broke off and remained silent for about half a minute. When he spoke again and gave me our instructions he was so unemotional that his voice frightened me. I remember thinking that it was like hearing a judge stating a decision that could never be revoked.' She sat on the edge of the desk and frowned around the room.

'Grant had made a decision, my dear. During that long pause he had sentenced Miss Reilly to death, not because she was a criminal, but because she had rejected him in the most emphatic way possible. She had shown her loathing by committing murder to escape from him. I think a man with Grant's ego would decide to kill his Paddy when he realized how deep her hatred of him was.'

'So, he makes his decision and works out the whole plan in thirty seconds, darling. That takes some believing, because he has to order a car, buy a necktie on his way to Castle Landon, and strangle the woman in exact imitation of Alban's methods. You must be wrong, but we can check on the car angle here and now.' Boris picked up the house telephone. 'Orel here, Sergeant Abbot. Please put me through to the transport officer. I see. Thanks all the same.' He lowered the phone irritably. 'They go off duty at half past twelve today.'

'And you now believe the old man is on his way to Wales to cry on George's shoulder. Also possible, I suppose, but highly unlikely, because they've never been really close. Even when George was a boy, neither Grant nor his wife showed him affection, and I don't suppose he and his father really know each other at all. Strange that, isn't it, Ruth? Why adopt a child, if you don't need its love? Obviously all the old brute wanted was to have somebody with his own name on the board of directors.'

'Then if he isn't going to George, where has he gone, Boris? Even if you don't believe that he killed Miss Reilly, we have to find him, darling. The chances are that that letter about you is in his pocket and we know he's in a state of shock. Grant might do anything with it.'

'Yes, Ruth, anything at all. He might be on his way to the Soviet embassy in London, in which case there is nothing to be done except admit that I'm finished.' Boris spoke without any emotion. 'But my guess is that Byrne is right and he is contemplating suicide. Either that, or driving aimlessly around to try and straighten out his thoughts.'

'Then let's see if Byrne is right.' Ruth dialled emergency and asked for the police. 'Traffic control please. I want to know if there has been an accident on the Pennines involving a black Rover Three Litre during the last hour. Thank you.' She replaced the phone and shook her head. 'No suicide so far, and though Grant may be driving aimlessly around, as you say, can we chance it? If he told George about you what would happen?'

'I haven't a clue, Ruth. George once thought of me as a friend, but that probably ended when I banged down the phone on him. Also, though he's very keen on penal reform and championing the underdogs, I don't imagine that George would regard an ex-secret policeman as someone to be helped and protected.' Boris eased back his chair and stood up. The possibility of Grant's suicide had seemed like a godsend, but it was not to be. He had to find Ernest Grant and force him to hand over that letter.

'No, I don't know how George would react, but you're right in saying I can't sit back and take chances. Your murder theory may be unlikely but he could be on his way to George, and I'll have to go after him.' He pulled Ruth to him and kissed her. 'I'm going on my own, though. You're going to stay and wait for me in Daneville, because I'm not having you involved in my troubles any more.'

'Like hell you're not, Boris.' She drew away and stood by the door. 'You're not the only person who wants to be paid because there's a slight matter of five thousand pounds owing to me. I also happen to be in love with you and we're in this together. Unless Grant's phobia about driving is a complete fabrication he'll probably go slowly and we should catch him before he reaches George. But he's got a long start, so let's get after him.'

Ernest Grant's fear of motoring on the open road was certainly real enough, but he was forcing himself to drive very fast indeed and he hummed to steady his nerves.

'Come back, Paddy Reilly, to Ballyjamesduff . . .' That song would always haunt him, he thought as he blasted a small van out of his way with the horn. He and Paddy had laughed about it once. They'd said that she'd never come back to him for the simple reason that they would never be apart. Then Madge's father had made his proposition, he'd left Paddy and the ballad had gone out of his mind.

'Come back, Paddy Reilly, to me . . .' He'd been lying half-conscious in hospital when he heard the words again. A fool of a nurse had turned on the radio to try to cheer him up when all he had wanted to do was to lie in peace and try to persuade himself that Madge's death had been an accident. His stroke had left him too weak to reach out and switch the radio off, and the tune had gone lilting on and on to bring back the past and torture him. Before the last verse was reached he had made his insane decision to find Paddy again.

Poor Madge, poor Paddy; two women who had died on his account. One became alcoholic because he did not love her and the other had been destroyed by fate because she had hated him and been incapable of mercy and forgiveness.

But was he capable of love, or was George right when he had once said that he merely wanted Paddy back to salve his own conscience? Megalomania was a word George had once used, and maybe it was the correct one. His mother's brother had died raving in the county asylum.

Drive carefully, though. You must learn the truth, or go

completely insane, but don't kill yourself. His hands were sweaty and he gripped the steering wheel tightly as the car shot from under a bridge and the side wind caught it again. He had had to go and identify Madge's body in the morgue, and body had been a polite way to describe it. What he had seen and smelled was stuff; burned, broken hideous stuff that they had produced in a metal drawer for his inspection. There had been no face to speak of, though a tang of alcohol still lingered amid the stench of anti-septic and corruption and only a mole on her neck and a wedding ring told him that Madge had finally left him. She'd threatened to do so many times over the years, but not once had he believed that she had the courage to keep her promises. But she had done so in the end and he would never know whether her death had been suicide or caused by drink.

Careful, now. The motorway exit was coming up and he pulled over behind a lorry belching diesel fumes. As he turned the wheel he felt the revolver in his pocket press against the arm-rest and he remembered how it had jerked in his hand when he shattered the lock of Paddy's bungalow.

Don't think about that, though. Concentrate on getting there safely, and don't have an accident because you must learn the truth today. God condemned Paddy to death, but you have to know what instruments He used.

With the speed reduced to forty miles an hour the car was almost silent apart from the tick of the clock and voices began to creep into his memory. Mrs Renton's voice on the telephone tell-ing him that Paddy hated him enough to commit murder, and the voices that had been recorded in error on George's tape machine. Both of them distressed him and Sir Ernest Grant raised his own voice to drive them away. 'Come back, Paddy Reilly, to Ballyjames-duff. Come back, Paddy Reilly, to me.'

Chapter Sixteen

'This is the first spectacular country I have seen since leaving Russia.' Ruth was driving and Boris watched the rugged landscapes spread out around them. But though he spoke pleasantly, he was only making conversation and his mood was savage. For two-thirds of the journey he had felt some hopes and had kept tensing in his seat whenever a black Rover appeared in front of them. But now they were far into Wales and his hopes had dwindled to almost nothing. Either they were on a wild-goose chase or Sir Ernest's fears of fast driving were feigned and he had been given too long a start. By now he might have told George all about him.

How would George react to the story, he wondered. Would a kindly disposition and their past friendship persuade him to keep quiet? Probably not, so how should he play his cards if George decided to inform against him? Plead, grovel, threaten to expose Sir Ernest, or merely shrug and accept defeat? Probably the latter because he was very, very tired of running.

Boris frowned at Ruth out of the corner of his eye. He loved her; the moment when he had woken up in the morning and found her beside him had been one of the happiest he had ever known, but how he wished she had not insisted on coming with him. If defeat was on the cards he did not want her to witness his humiliation.

'You like our hills?' Ruth was partly Welsh and she smiled proprietarily. They were climbing a long winding pass flanked by crags and scree shoots. The sun was setting, but the moon was appearing through the clouds, and whenever the crags parted a range of big mountains could be seen in the north. 'I thought Russia was mainly flat.'

'Most of it is, but we have mountains, too. When I was young we once went for a holiday in the Caucasus.' Boris thought of the tent perched below the snow line, the smell of flowers and woodsmoke and the eagles wheeling around the twin peaks of 'Two-headed Usbah'. Life had been good till the day he had walked into the professor's study and found Peter Vanin waiting for him like an old-maidish spider. It would be good again providing Sir Ernest Grant honoured their bargain.

They might know that soon enough. Boris consulted the map. Ruth might be right in believing Sir Ernest had gone to George. But if so it would be sympathy, not absolution that he would be after and before long Harry Alban must be captured and found responsible for all three murders. Grant was not a killer, but he was a very disturbed man who suffered from delusions. All that concerned Boris was that he kept his word and remained silent.

'About twenty-five miles to go, Ruth.' The head of the pass was behind and the road had begun to wind down towards a coastal plain. In the north the hills were falling away, but bigger mountains could be seen in the south-west. At the end of the plain lay Port Olwyn where they must leave the main road and cross the estuary by a causeway. According to the map the road was a very minor one from there on. It wound across the fells, serving several farms and hamlets and took some eighteen miles against the railway's ten to reach Bryncir where George's cottage was situated.

'Boris, I've been thinking about Grant's motives ever since we started out and I believe I've got it at last.' They had reached the plain and Ruth accelerated along the level road though she had given up hope of catching the Rover. 'You remember that he told Byrne he had injured George in some way and had to confide in him?'

'Naturally. We've been all over that and it's no proof that he killed Miss Reilly. Because she's dead he needs George's love and sympathy. Probably he also wants George to forgive him for being neglected as a child. Why should the woman's death bother George? He was against the old man looking for her from the word go.' Boris was still studying the route. Time was getting on, the sun was dwindling to a red smudge on the sea, the evening star was out and the lights of Port Olwyn lay ahead. 'If you're right and Grant did murder her, he's done George a good turn. Maybe he's gone to Bryncir for congratulations. That's a logical possibility and they say there's method in madness.'

'For God's sake stop airing your knowledge of English plati-tudes, Boris.' Ruth had sensed his mood for a long time and tried to ignore it, but now she was angry. 'And don't be so bloody rude, either. For some reason you didn't want me to come with you, but there's no need to sneer before I've even tried to tell you what I think the truth is. If you'd use a little logic yourself, you'd realize that Miss Reilly's death may have injured George terribly, though George does not know it.'

'Sorry, darling. I didn't mean to be rude, but I'm quite sure Grant is not a murderer. All I can worry about is the letter and whether he tells George about me.' Boris laid down the map and looked at the buildings closing around them. Port Olwyn was not a popular resort but like most seaside towns it looked dead and depressing in the off season. They passed a deserted caravan site, two chapels and a cinema-cum-bingo hall and turned into the main street which terminated at a roundabout and an almost empty car park. Beyond the roundabout lay the station. Three freshly painted buildings with a clock tower and a line of hoardings. In the light of a street lamp Boris read that the Port Olwyn and Bryncir Railway provided a summer service through ten miles of spectacular mountain scenery. 'Please tell me what your idea is, Ruth.'

'George was six years old when the Grants adopted him; a pretty late age and neither of them showed him affection.' Ruth switched on her headlights. The road over the causeway was dark and narrow and hemmed in between the sea wall and the railway embankment. 'It seems odd of them to have taken on the responsibility of a child if they didn't want its love.'

'They were odd people, Ruth. As I've said before old Grant adopted George to keep his own name in the business and as he had no affection for his wife, she might have resented George's presence. Isn't that feasible?' Boris was only mildly interested and part of his thoughts were on the railway. The causeway curved sharply as it reached the bank of the estuary and the line and the road parted company on a level crossing flanked with speed restriction notices. Very necessary notices, he considered. If one of George's elderly locomotives took that bend at much more than the permitted ten miles an hour she'd jump the rails.

'Not really feasible, Boris. I can understand Lady Grant's feelings towards the boy, but not why Sir Ernest should have neglected him. If he wanted George to take over the firm one day, surely he would have found time to train and influence him? You've told me how he dominates his employees. Wouldn't he have wanted to mould his adopted son more than anyone else?'

'You've got a point there.' The railway was stretching straight up into the hills and Boris could see its single track glinting in the moonlight. Had George been given a model train when he was young, he thought? Had loneliness and rejection by the Grants turned his toys into love objects and produced a passion for railways which was his main interest in life?

'Yes it's certainly strange that Grant himself should have kept away from the boy. By all accounts he gave him hardly any attention at all. George once used the phrase "I was procured" when describing his adoption to me.'

'I think George could be wrong about that.' After crossing the railway the road had started to undulate gently across the fells. It was very narrow; little better than a lane and sheep were grazing along the unfenced verges. High above and to the north the vast pipes of a hydro-electric installation were plunging down towards the coast.

'Grant may have loved George very much indeed, but avoided him because he was frightened to show the boy affection, darling. Perhaps the very sight of George caused his parents pain in different ways. Lady Grant was tortured by jealousy and her husband by love.'

'The penny's dropped and you could be an extremely clever girl, Ruth.' Boris watched the glittering railway lines and he thought of a little boy playing obsessively with his toys because a man and a woman fought to conceal their feelings towards him.

'You believe that the Grants are blood relations, don't you? You also think you know what the confession will be. That Sir Ernest has come here to tell his own son that he murdered his mother.'

It was possible. George Grant might not have been procured, as he said, or even adopted in the strict sense of the word. He could have been sent as a gift because he was Ernest Grant's natural child . . . Grant's and Paddy Reilly's. Boris stared fixedly through the windscreen while he considered the theory. They were high up, the road zigzagging between hamlets and isolated farms and at every mile the country grew wilder. The lights of Port Olwyn were out of sight and big mountains dominated the horizons; their peaks black and hostile in the gloom.

Yes, quite possible. Grant had not known that Paddy was preg-

nant when he deserted her and out of pride or perversity she did
not tell him she had borne his child when they met by chance in
the restaurant. But in time she might have wearied of the boy or
begun to dislike him because he reminded her of her former lover.
She had handed George over to some institution or foster parent
and instructed them to get in touch with his father. Probably it
was made clear to Grant that she would reclaim the child if he
attempted to contact her.

Ernest Grant would have collected his son immediately. He was
said to be a man of family pride and would have been elated to have
someone of his own flesh and blood in the firm. He had adopted
George, but his wife must have insisted that the boy's true identity
remained a secret and for once her wishes had been respected.

'TREFLYS HALT – Summer services to Bryncir and Port Olwyn.'
The road had been running parallel to a curving viaduct and now
crossed the line at a tiny station that stood quite alone with not
another building in sight. The crossing was without gates and
a forlorn notice: CLOSED FOR THE WINTER was displayed on the
ticket office.

Out of loyalty to his wife, or more probably because George
reminded him of the woman he had loved and wronged, Sir Ernest
had kept himself aloof from his son. But after Lady Grant had
died, and the stroke had come, Grant had decided to find Paddy
Reilly again.

Possibly not only for his own sake either. Boris could imagine
how the old man would have planned his surprise. 'I've found
her, George, I'm going to marry her, and you can stop looking so
miserable about it. You'll be our best man, son, because my future
wife happens to be your mother.'

But if Ruth was right in other ways: if Grant had murdered the
woman when he discovered how deep her loathing of him was,
how would he react? Would they find him standing before George
with tears in his eyes and the tic racking his face as he poured out
his confession? 'Must forgive me, boy . . . must understand . . .
couldn't help myself . . . need your love so badly now . . . You can
feel pity for those criminals you visit, so pity me, your own father.'

Yes, Ruth's theory was feasible, but Boris could not feel com-

pletely convinced. Probably Grant was back at his house in Daneville and all they'd find at Bryncir would be George and some of
his fellow enthusiasts happily tinkering on one of their beloved
locomotives.

They would know soon. The car was approaching a saucer of
ground set between three hills and at the end of the saucer lay a
cluster of rectangular blocks which Boris had first imagined were
gigantic boulders. But as the headlamps drew nearer, he could
see that they were buildings standing empty and forlorn with not
a light showing anywhere. George had told him Bryncir's history
and it was a depressing one. The railway had been built in the 1850s
to serve several slate quarries and by the turn of the century the
village had become a prosperous place with over a thousand inhabitants. But between the wars tiled roofs had come into fashion and
the demand for slate dwindled. One by one the quarries cut down
production and finally closed, one after another the families moved
away because there was no work to support them. Finally no more
trains had come snorting up from Port Olwyn and Bryncir died.

Now George and his colleagues had reopened the line and hoped
to run it as a tourist attraction. Boris sensed that the project was
doomed to failure. As the details of the deserted village became
clearer, he saw that Bryncir was not merely sad and depressing,
there was something sinister about it, too, and he could almost
imagine the ghosts of its former inhabitants peering out at them
from the empty houses. Most of the roofs were intact, but the
doors and windows had been stripped away and many of the walls
were overgrown by creepers. They made him think of ornamental
yew trees that had been trained into the shapes of buildings.

There was the chapel with the branches of a big tree growing
through the roof, there was the school and a line of terraced
cottages, there was a largish house that might have belonged to
the minister or one of the quarry managers. There at last were
lights.

'You were right in one thing, Ruth. Whether Grant is a murderer or not, he's here.' The road skirted a cobbled square before
continuing out of the village and two cars were parked in the
centre of the square. George's elderly shooting brake, coated with

mud and dust, and Sir Ernest's black Rover, looking elegant and urbane amid the squalor of the ruins.

'The station must be beyond that passage.' Ruth drew up and Boris climbed out of the car. The lights were coming from the end of an alley and on the wind which was blowing more strongly he smelled something which brought back a score of memories. Hot metal and oil, furnace smoke and water vapour; the smell of a locomotive with steam up.

'I'll do the talking, Ruth.' He led the way forward. 'Don't say anything about your suspicions to the Grants. Just keep quiet and let me get your cheque and my letter.'

The alley led out on to a patch of waste land and beyond that lay the tiny terminus of the railway. The station building had lights glowing in its entrance hall and one window and another light was coming from an engine shed to the right where the line ended. Protruding from the entrance of the shed they could see the front end of a high-funnelled 2-4-0 locomotive. She looked very fine in her apple-green paint and brasswork and steam was hissing from the safety valves. Boris recognized *Cambrian Rose*, George's pride and joy which had been saved from the scrap yard and rebuilt. Probably he had been testing the boiler tubes under pressure when Sir Ernest arrived.

'Yes, you do the talking, Boris.' Ruth followed him towards the station. The waste land had been cleared to provide a car park, small trees and bushes lay piled in heaps to be burned and the surface was scarred by bulldozers. 'But you've got to break old Grant down, darling. You must make him confess to murder. Please stop and listen for a moment.'

He was walking very quickly and Ruth's high-heeled shoes stumbled over the rough ground while she tried to keep up with him. 'That letter and Grant's promise don't mean a thing, but if he admits that he murdered Miss Reilly we've got him and he'd never dare to inform against you. But the point is that George must never know. We must talk to Grant alone somehow. I said listen to me, Boris.' She caught up with him as they neared the lighted window and he did stop, but not because of her. Ruth followed his stare and her body became quite rigid.

As might have been expected both the Grants were in the room. George stood with his back against the wall, his fists were clenched and he was craning forward with arms slightly outstretched. His face looked angry and dangerous above the grizzled beard and he made Ruth think of the Minotaur preparing to charge. But it was Sir Ernest Grant who provided the real menace.

The last time they had seen the old man he had appeared broken and pathetic, and Michael Byrne had reported that his condition had been the same that morning. But like a chameleon Deadly Earnest had changed again. He sat stiffly on a bench and his face was imperious and without any tremor. His revolver was pointing at George's heart and his hand was quite steady.

Chapter Seventeen

'Keep well down and move quietly. He'll shoot if he hears us.' They had crouched below the level of the window and Boris began to edge across to the station entrance. He felt deep anxiety for George and humility towards Ruth, because it seemed that she had been right about everything.

Ernest Grant's insanity was divided between remorse and megalomania and they swung backwards and forwards in his brain like the strides of a pendulum. Guilt and imagined love had driven him to seek Paddy Reilly out. Fury at the knowledge that she had killed Paulson to escape from him had promoted her murder. Then remorse had taken over again and he had come to George to confess and gain forgiveness.

Obviously George had not forgiven him. George had been told about his parentage and he must have recoiled in horror when he realized who Miss Reilly was and why she had died. Grant had been rejected by another person whose love he craved and unless Boris could intervene efficiently, Ernest Grant would have killed both the mother and the son.

He was going to intervene all right. Boris's fingers touched a jagged lump of slate and closed around it. Relief and gratitude joined his other emotions because fate was on his side at last.

An honourable motive for silencing Grant had been provided, the weapon placed in his hand and Sir Ernest's death need never trouble his conscience. Who would condemn him for killing a maniac to save George's life?

They could not be seen from the window now and he stood up and walked into the entrance hall with Ruth behind him. In front of them was the barrier leading to the platforms, on the right the ticket office and a counter for selling postcards and souvenirs, on the left the doors of the toilets and a door marked STATION MASTER, STRICTLY PRIVATE. Boris moved towards that door, circling round the centre of the hall which was railed off to form a miniature museum of the railway's history. Trestles supported nameplates of scrapped locomotives, a silver trowel that had been used by a royal personage to cut the first sod when the line was begun, and a collection of signal flags and rattles and other pieces of equipment. Behind the trestles, a raised panel displayed prints and photographs while on the floor larger exhibits were positioned. A plate-layer's barrow, an early weighing machine, two locomotive funnels, a connecting rod and a small closed truck labelled 'Coffin Wagon Number 1'. Boris recalled that George had mentioned its restoration with pride some months ago. Unless he was lucky, George might be needing the services of a coffin himself.

The door to the station master's quarters was unlocked and it opened soundlessly on well-oiled hinges. Beyond lay a long narrow passage that smelled of damp leather and was stacked with piles of carriage seats awaiting renovation. Inch by inch Boris and Ruth crept past them towards the half-open door behind which the Grants were confronting each other.

'Shall we conclude the arrangement, then?' There must be a third person in the room and Ruth almost cried out as she heard the dead speak. The voice was Eric Paulson's and though he sounded as if he were suffering from a heavy cold, she recognized it clearly.

'Six thousand pounds in two equal amounts is the sum we decided was fair, so if you will let me have your cheques, I will lock them in the safe.' There was a pause and Ruth pressed her hand against her mouth to stop herself screaming. It was certainly

Eric's voice, but how could it be? It was she who had discovered his body. She watched Boris edge on with the rock in his hand, but remained motionless and quite unable to follow him.

'The sum was agreed in principle, but how do I know that the bargain will be kept?' There was a pause and then George Grant spoke. Like Eric Paulson's, his voice was muffled and indistinct. 'The cheques are to be post-dated till the first of next month, but once they are cashed we have no guarantee whatsoever. I suggest that the date should be extended to the end of the year.'

'You have my word that my side of the bargain will be honoured, sir.' Eric Paulson had prided himself on being a man of principle and he was clearly offended. While he spoke Ruth heard the sound of a heavy door creaking open. 'Stick to our arrangement; six thousand pounds to be collected on the first of next month and I shall tell my client that I have met with no success whatsoever and am dropping the case. But unless I receive payment here and now, Mr Grant, I shall pick up the telephone and give your father Miss Reilly's address.' Eric Paulson's words changed to a scream, there was a crash of metal and then a brief silence.

'Don't lie to me again, George.' Sir Ernest Grant was speaking. 'You had this contraption on you when you went to Paulson's office and owing to a faulty switch it recorded his murder. I suppose the mechanism stopped when you threw him into the safe.' Boris had reached the end of the passage and he peered through the gap between the door and its post.

The Grants were in exactly the same positions as before. Sir Ernest on the bench and George standing beside another door to the right. He was wearing overalls and black oil coated his hands like rubber gloves.

'If you must play with toys, my boy, make sure that they are in working order in future.' The old man slipped the little tape recorder into his pocket. 'Not that there is any future for you, George. You bribed Paulson to stop me finding Paddy, but his word wasn't good enough and you murdered him. And because of that, Paddy's dead and you're responsible.' His hand was tightening on the trigger of the revolver and Boris braced himself to hurl the door open. 'Your craving for affection . . . your morbid fears that a third person would come between us are as much responsible for her death as that escaped maniac. You kept me away from the only woman I ever loved, and when I found her it was too late.'

'I repeat that I did not kill Eric Paulson.' George spoke for the first time since Boris had entered the passage. 'You have my word, Father.'

'There's no need to go on lying to me, my boy, because I'm not blameless, either.' Grant slightly relaxed his grip on the gun. 'I wanted to play God and surprise you with a revelation and I didn't realize just how insanely strong your feelings were. If I hadn't been blind . . . if I'd only told you the truth about Paddy . . . you'd have welcomed her home, and the three of us would have been so happy together.' The wind was becoming more violent while he spoke. Its gusts rattled the window and from the engine shed came the bellow of the locomotive blowing off steam.

'But I'm going to keep my secret, George. I have to kill you, but I don't want to torture you and you'll never know just what a terrible thing you've done.' He frowned as a thought struck him. 'And maybe Paddy had to die to punish us; to deprive us of her love. Perhaps Harry Alban was an instrument of vengeance and fate led him to her. In any case, we're two evil men and we've got to pay for what we've done; your murderous jealousy and my cruelty in the past. There's one bullet for you, son, and another for me. Doesn't that seem fair to you? What a fool I've been. Blind to love in the past and untrusting now.' His finger was tight on the trigger again and Boris raised the rock. 'Orel and the Renton woman suspected that Paddy had killed Paulson to escape from me, and before I heard your tape, I almost believed them. I thought she might have hated me enough to do that.'

'They were right, Father, and she did hate you enough.' George's voice was so intense and strained that for a moment Ruth, who could not see into the room, imagined that the tape recorder had been switched on. 'Your sweet Paddy Reilly killed Eric Paulson and I saw her do it. She was standing beside him when he opened the safe door and all it took was a single push. Such a small woman, but so determined, so very strong.'

'You're lying, boy. Paddy wouldn't harm anybody; not my

Paddy.' Grant spoke with complete conviction, but the revolver trembled in his hand. 'And it's a foolish lie, George. If it were true you'd have gone straight to the police. You had no reason to shield her.'

'Hadn't I?' George's body relaxed and ignoring the gun he stepped forward and leaned against a table in the centre of the room. 'Isn't a son bound to protect his own mother?'

'Yes, I know how you hoped to surprise me. I know that Paddy Reilly was my mother.' George no longer looked dangerous, but rather crushed and pathetic. 'Paulson never guessed our relationship. He telephoned me and said that he had located the woman you were looking for. At the moment her one wish was to be left in peace and she had offered him three thousand pounds, her entire life savings, to be left in peace.

'Eric Paulson was a persuasive man. He put it to me that though the woman was desperate to avoid you now, her feelings might change in time. If they did and you married her, I could be a heavy financial loser at your death and it was in my interest to keep the two of you apart. Paulson was prepared to drop the case if I would add a further three thousand to her offer.' George stared down at the top of the table as if picturing the events reflected on its surface.

'I didn't want you to remarry anybody, Father, and I jumped at the offer. I went to Paulson's office with the cheque made out and after all those years I met Paddy Reilly again. The whole room seemed to revolve when I first set eyes on her and for a moment I thought I had lost my senses. But when I had pulled myself together I knew that there was no mistake. That woman was my mother and I could no more have informed against her than I could have . . .' He shook his head unable to find a comparison.

'I still believe you're lying, George.' Sir Ernest spoke firmly but it was clear that his doubts were growing and the pistol hung loosely in his grasp. 'You loved your mother when you were a child. Naturally you would shield her, even if she had committed murder, but why didn't you stop her and make her see reason? Why didn't you persuade her to come back to me of her own free will? After you recognized her, you must have guessed who I was.

We were your parents, my boy, your own father and mother. You should have moved heaven and earth to bring us together. I needed Paddy so much, George . . . I needed both of you.'

'Love! You think that I loved her?' George's eyes were closed and his lips were drawn back over his teeth. 'You're a fool, Father, and you still don't understand a thing. You never listened to me when I was young, but you're going to listen now. I hated my mother . . . I loathed and feared her, and I still do.

'After she'd slammed the safe door on Paulson, I pushed her aside and tugged at the handle in the senseless hope that the lock hadn't caught. Then she took hold of my arm and she spoke to me as if I was still a child. She told me to stop being a fool because there was nothing I could do to help Paulson. His secretary was abroad and it would be days before anybody opened the safe and found his body. She made me swear that I would keep quiet and never mention the whole horrible business to anyone.' George opened his eyes and Boris saw something he had never noticed before. They were very small, sharp, deep-set eyes, and like Paddy Reilly's they did not seem to belong to the rest of his face. 'And I obeyed her – I protected that woman because I was still frightened of her. Isn't that silly, Father? A middle-aged man being frightened of his own mother whom he had not seen since he was six years old.

'I ran away from reality for a time. I took a long weekend and came down here to try to put what had happened out of my thoughts. I walked on the hills, I tinkered with *Cambrian Rose* and I sat in this room and tried and tried to forget everything. But quite the opposite happened. After a time I saw quite clearly what my life had been.'

He stared around the room with its dark, varnished woodwork, bare furnishings and the walls hung with old prints and posters and railway timetables. 'I also realized what my purpose in life was. Do you know why Paddy Reilly sent me to that children's home in Sussex and told them to inform you I was there, Father? I suppose I must have known once, but it had been driven deep into my subconscious: defensive withdrawal is what some pundits call the phenomenon.

'But on the second evening after Paulson's death, sitting on that bench as you are now, I saw all my childhood spread out like a strip cartoon. My mother hated me because I reminded her of you. She couldn't bear the sight or sound of us. She felt physically sick if we touched her or even came near her. That is why we were made to suffer so much. That is why I became one of those instruments of fate that you believe in. Why I had a vision which told me to open a door and join a crusade.' George fingered his necktie and smiled at his father. The dark cap and overalls and the black oil staining his hands gave him a strangely priest-like and funereal appearance. That is why I strangled Paddy with one of these.'

'You – you – you.' Boris had been too stunned by the revelation to intervene and Ernest Grant had fired. But the bullet went wide and the revolver had dropped from his grasp and fallen to the floor. 'Why, George? How could you? Your own mother – in cold blood – worked out and planned – imitating that crazed monster's method to protect yourself. For the love of God, why, George?'

'For God, Father, but not in cold blood.' George Grant raised his left wrist to the light to show a pattern of old scars. 'God has made a hell for those who torture children; the fire, the millstone, the worm that never dies. All those noises I heard sitting here that evening. The crash of the safe door, her voice as I tugged at it, Paulson's body threshing against the metal. They brought back all the other things I had forced myself to forget. That safe reminded me of the cupboard under the stairs where she used to lock me in if I cried or played too noisily.

'"Brat . . . brat . . . Grant brat. Child with a devil that has to be driven out of him."' George's voice had risen to a shrill falsetto and Boris and Ruth recognized the voice of Paddy Reilly.

'"You'd try to stop me, would you, brat? You'd dare to resist your own mother. Under the stairs with you, then. No, I'll do better than that, George. Sic him, Rover. Get your teeth into the little beast, there's my good boy."' The words changed to a dog's snarl and when George spoke again, his voice had deepened, but his eyes had lost their sharpness and saliva was dribbling down his beard.

'So many ways she had to torture us, Father. The cupboard, the leather strap, a hand pressed against the fire bars, the teeth of a terrier.' He held up his wrist again. 'Worst of all, humiliation and lack of love because the boy reminded her of you.

'The boy had a present once. The landlady gave it to him; a little toy train painted Midland Red. Mummy sent it to the church jumble sale. Presents are for nice children, she said. Not for bed-wetting cretins spawned by Ernest Grant.

'"Dirty mindless ape who can't dress himself properly."' Once more the scolding, high-pitched tones rang out. '"Run and fetch the strap, George, because it's lesson time. We're going to teach that imbecile how to tie his tie."'

'Tie . . . tie . . . tie. Tie it round Mummy's neck, George.' Apart from a cockney accent, the voice was identical to George's natural voice, but George's lips were not moving.

'Tighter than that, George, much, much tighter. Hurt Mummy . . . Make naughty Mummy die.' The door beside George had opened and into the room came Harry Alban, the Hangman.

*

Boris and Ruth never heard Alban speak again, but they had the odd feeling that he did not need to speak because George spoke for him. The two men stood close together by the table, and without George's beard they would have been easily recognizable as twins. Also, though George was tanned and physically healthy and the escaped prisoner had a pallid complexion, Boris sensed that Harry Alban was the dominant partner because George had been infected by his mania and obeyed him like a ventriloquist's dummy.

Sometimes George spoke in his normal voice and appeared almost rational, sometimes Miss Reilly's hectoring tones poured from his mouth. Now and again a child sobbed and whimpered in self-pity and they could hardly understand him.

But the gist of the story was clear enough. Paddy Reilly did not know she was pregnant when Ernest Grant deserted her, but seven months later she gave birth to twins. She had inherited a little money of her own and for some reason – possibly pride, possibly defiance – she decided to keep the children, though the very sight of them reminded her of the man she loathed and one boy was subnormal. Perhaps the beating she had received at Grant's hands had had something to do with his condition.

To a woman as proud and determined as Miss Reilly, a child that wetted its bed, that dribbled at the mouth, whose greasy finger marks were always to be found on her highly polished furniture was a challenge to be met and she went to work with a will. The sins of the father were certainly visited on Grant's children, and as George had said the stair cupboard, the strap and the fire bars were just a few methods of correction. Harry received the brunt of her anger, but George shared his brother's misery in his mind and suffered physically whenever he tried to intervene.

'We wanted Mummy to love us. But she never kissed us once in all our lives, did she, Harry? Wicked, cruel Mummy. I made myself forget her when we were sent away, but you were braver and wiser than me. You never forgot anything, did you, Harry Bear?' There was something obscene in the childish accents tripping from George's lips and his hand reached out and fondled Alban's.

The twins were six years old when Paddy Reilly finally decided to get rid of them. Her dislike had increased, her money was starting to run out and they were becoming big, strong boys. Once when she took the strap to Harry, George had picked up a table knife and threatened her and that made up her mind. During the chance meeting with Ernest Grant in the restaurant he had said how much he would have loved to have a son and George's future was provided for. She might have considered letting Grant have Harry, too, as a cruel memento, but probably pride prevented that. Not even the man who had fathered her children must know that she had produced a half-wit.

So George was handed over to a children's home with the promise that his father would collect him as soon as he was contacted, and Harry was taken to St Pancras station and left in the first train listed on the departure board. He had a ticket to St Albans in his pocket, and lodged in his simple brain was the threat of severe punishment if he revealed anything about his past.

George managed to forget his childhood after the Grants adopted him. At least his conscious mind forgot, but deep down behind consciousness, the memories festered and they came bubbling out like sewer gas on the day he met his mother in Paulson's office.

Harry did not forget. Fear and the craving for love were always with him, and by an unfortunate coincidence the orphanage matron bore a strong physical resemblance to his mother. Mrs Oliver was a kind woman, she earned his love, but after a time Harry's drooling, dog-like devotion became too much to bear. She rejected him, she struck him when he followed her about, one day he tried to kill her, and their paths separated.

Harry was twenty-five when he saw his mother and Mrs Oliver again. He met them quite by chance in a shop in the East End of London and the curious thing was that they were both sharing a single body. It was also curious that the shopkeeper kept referring to them as Mrs Jackson, but Harry saw through the deception and he followed the little jaunty figure down the street. She might deceive other people but not him. That was Matron who had kept driving him away from her when he needed her love so much. That was Mummy who had whipped him and locked him in the dark and almost strangled him with his necktie because he couldn't manage to tie it himself.

Mrs Ellen Jackson, the wife of a bus conductor and mother of three perfectly happy children had started to head home across a stretch of waste land; Harry Alban loosened his tie and the Hangman claimed his first victim.

'Harry and I didn't recognize each other when we first met in his cell at Seamont, Father.' George spoke in his natural voice, and from the bench Sir Ernest Grant sat watching his sons. 'But we knew that we had something in common, didn't we, Harry? You were a convict, I was a prison visitor, but we both felt that there was a bond between us . . . some task that we had to share and carry out together. But then, after I saw Mummy again . . . after she killed the detective . . . after she made me promise not to tell on her, it all started to come back and when I was down here, I realized that you must be little Harry Bear.' Word by word the child's voice returned. 'Yes, I knew you were my brother. I knew that you were unhappy because people had locked you up under the stairs again. I decided to help you to run away, and I was so clever and lucky, wasn't I? You thought we might have to wait for

days and days, didn't you? But I knew better, Harry. God . . . Baby
Jesus was with us and the very first evening was foggy. It was all as
easy as tiddlywinks.

'But you were a clever one as well, Harry Bear. When I'd got
you safely tucked away down here, you explained everything and
told me just what it was we had to do together.' For a brief instant
George's voice became adult. 'We had no toys, Father. The woman
never gave us any toys, so we had to make up games. I used to
pretend that Harry was a teddy bear.

'And Harry is such a clever bear and he explained how the
woman can come back to life and change her appearance ever so
slightly. How we have to be on our guard against her all the time
and learn to spot her before she can hurt us.' He smiled at his
brother who stood silently beside him with his shoulders hunched
and face sunk in shadow.

'I hardly recognized Mummy in the first woman I killed. I had
to force myself to strangle her; partly for practice, and partly to
throw the blame on Harry so that no one would suspect me; a
red herring, they call it. But the second was easier. I watched her
sitting in that public house and I knew her at once. I had no trouble
at all.' A child's eyes glowed with triumph and saliva dribbled down
a man's greying beard.

'Finally there was Mummy . . . our real mummy in her own
flesh who hadn't tried to disguise herself one little bit. I hadn't
wanted to kill her so soon, Father. I wanted to wait and pluck up
courage, but when I heard you talking on the phone to that Mrs
Renton, I knew I had to get there before you. How she screamed
when she saw me come in through the back door with the tie in
my hand. How she pleaded with me when I caught her in the
passage. Mummy'd never suspected that Harry was the Hangman
till that moment.'

The smile vanished and George shook his head. 'I felt so happy
and proud when it was over, but so foolish when Harry told me
that she would come alive again and we could never relax . . . never
really be free of her. Well, what are you going to do, Father? You
won't try to kill us, will you? Not your own children, surely? We
haven't done you any harm, so please go away and don't tell any-

one that we're here.' Tears were dribbling down George's cheeks to join the saliva moistening his beard.

'You've nothing to fear from me, George.' Ernest Grant lifted the revolver from the floor. 'My love for an evil woman made you what you are and I'm to blame for everything. Paddy and I must have been related as I thought, and our tainted genes merged in you. But I want to rest for a bit, boys, because I'm tired, terribly tired.' The muzzle of the gun was almost touching his lips and the nervous tremor jerked at his cheek.

'I must sleep now, so goodbye, George. Goodbye, Harry. Good night, my two fine sons.'

'No, don't shoot.' Boris did not know what made him cry out. He wanted Grant's death as much as anything in the world, he had once considered murdering him and now the old man was about to die of his own accord. Behind the door were two homicidal maniacs and his only thought should have been to get Ruth and himself to safety, call the police and then somehow lay hands on the papers in Grant's pocket. But all at once he felt as though Sir Ernest's life had been put in his charge and he had to save him from himself. He hurled open the door and threw the rock.

'Drop the pistol.' His aim had been good, the jagged lump of slate slammed against Grant's shoulder and threw him sideways. But Grant's grip did not loosen, and his mind hardly seemed to register the blow. He half-sat, half-lay on the bench with the muzzle in his mouth and he was still staring at his sons when he pulled the trigger.

Boris heard the explosion, and the voices bellowing at his side. He saw Sir Ernest's face disintegrate and he felt a stab of pain as Alban's hand flailed across his neck. But the feeling only lasted for a split second. Before his knees started to buckle, pain vanished; everything vanished. There was no light, no sound, no sensation. Only the void – nothing at all.

Chapter Eighteen

'Or . . . el, Boris Or . . . el.' Somebody was trying to attract his attention, but the owner of the voice was clearly mistaken, because his name was not Orel. He was Boris Dubassof and he was lying half-buried under a snowdrift in Berlin.

'Or . . . el, Or . . . el.' Why did the voice keep repeating a dead man's name? Orel must have died when the plane crashed and he had seen the flames roaring up into the sky. He was Boris Dubassof and it would have been much better if he had died with the others.

'Wake up, Or . . . el.' The voice had a very demanding quality and the words came in gasps which heightened their urgency. Soon he would open his eyes and look at the man who was calling to him, but not for a moment or two. The snow was soft and comfortable and he wanted to rest quietly and dream of the things that could have been. The life he might have had if Peter Vanin had not recruited him as an agent. The peace of death which that soft, comfortable snowdrift had denied him by breaking his fall.

'Or . . . el . . .' The urgency was too strong to be resisted and Boris opened his eyes. Reality returned slowly, but after a while the past slipped away and he realized that he was in the room at Bryncir station. Ruth was kneeling at his side, and a dribble of blood on the floor guided his eyes to the face of Sir Ernest Grant.

'Or . . . el . . . take these.' Grant's face was barely recognizable. There was a gaping hole in his cheek and the bullet had shattered his jaw. Broken teeth and bone fragments lay strewn around him like confetti.

'Please take . . .' With half his tongue torn to shreds it was a miracle that the old man could speak at all, but by some enormous effort of will he made the message clear and Boris saw two envelopes clutched in his hand.

'Must . . . pay debts.' The eyes flickered as Boris reached for the envelopes, and then closed. Sir Ernest had gone to join his Paddy on the long journey.

'Are you all right, Ruth? They didn't harm you, my darling?' Boris let her help him up from the floor. His head throbbed agonizingly and his feet felt as though they could barely support him. 'Where are they, though: George and Alban?'

'They've gone, Boris, but only a few seconds ago.' She led him over to a chair. 'I screamed and ran into the room after Alban stunned you and George grabbed hold of me. He wound a tie around my throat and Alban put Grant's gun against your forehead.' She nodded at the floor and Boris saw a striped necktie lying beside the table, but no sign of the revolver. 'George started to pull it tighter and tighter and then Alban suddenly put away the pistol and shook his head. George let go of me at once.'

'He had to let go of you, Ruth. They've no need to kill us. George and Harry are machines; radio receivers tuned to a single transmitter and the only person they must kill is their mother and her images.' Boris struggled to clear his thoughts and remember all that had happened. 'And Paddy Reilly is dead, isn't she? George strangled her, so the mad crusade is finally over. They'll probably give themselves up, but you'd better call the police.' He looked towards the telephone and saw that the wires had been torn out from the wall.

'No, Miss Reilly is not dead, Boris; not in their minds, at least. Don't you remember that George said she could never die?' Outside revolver shots rang out and a car engine started. Ruth crossed to the window and saw the lights of George's shooting brake moving away through the ruins.

'They talked about their plans before they left. They really do think of their mother as that monster Hercules fought. The Hydra that grows more heads as soon as one is struck off. They know they'll be caught and they're saving two bullets for themselves when that happens.'

'And before they're caught a lot of people could die.' Boris's brain was clearing and he tried to look into George and Harry's sick minds and picture the daemon that tortured and inspired them. George Grant had forced away his childhood terrors till he was a middle-aged man. But fate had led him to Alban's cell, fate had brought him face to face with Paddy Reilly again and his mania was released. Now the brothers were united in soul and purpose. Two crusaders fighting a menace which could never be destroyed, but must be struck down whenever it appeared.

'The Hydra; the multi-headed beast that has to be killed over and over again.' There was a map beside the window and Boris staggered over to it. 'They have to be stopped before they reach a main road junction, Ruth, and there are only two places where they can do that. Here, at the end of the Port Olwyn viaduct, and at this village to the north.' Through the window he saw that the headlights were out of Bryncir and branching across the fells. 'Yes, they're heading for Port Olwyn so all we have to do is find the nearest telephone and tell the police to block the lane. If the car can be spotted before it reaches Port Olwyn there's nothing to worry about. If not, it might be days before they're caught and in that time . . .'

Ordinary, commonplace, inoffensive women, Boris thought as he turned and hurried painfully out of the room and along the passage. Small, elderly women with fair hair, rather compact features and sharp, deeply-set eyes. Mrs Oliver, the hospital matron who had made the radio appeal telling Alban to give himself up and many, many others who were anonymous. Women coming home from work, doing their shopping, going to play bingo, visiting friends, or merely walking for pleasure. Women who might be doomed because they had one thing in common. They bore a close resemblance to Paddy Reilly and their faces belonged to the Hydra which had to be killed over and over again.

'We've ample time, though, and the police will stop them all right, Ruth. It's a good eighteen miles to the junction and the road winds all the way. It took you over half an hour to drive up, remember.' Their feet rang hollowly across the stretch of scarred ground outside the station. 'As soon as we find a farm with a telephone, they're trapped.' Side by side Boris and Ruth pounded on and their hopes increased till they reached the end of the alley; then faded. They had not realized the purpose of the revolver shots and Grant's Rover and Boris's Ford were leaning affectionately towards each other. Both cars had a flat front tyre.

'The last farm I noticed must have been a couple of miles back.

Even if we cut across the fells on foot, we'd never get there in time.' On the way to the station Ruth had not found the deserted village particularly sinister. But the wind had blown up into a gale: its gusts howled and sobbed through the ruins and she began to feel that the voices of Bryncir's dead were lamenting their defeat. 'How long will it take you to change the wheel, darling?'

'Too long probably, but it's all I can do.' Boris had taken a wheel brace from the Ford's boot, but he suddenly let it fall to the ground. The fury of the wind had reminded him of another sound and it told him that hope was not completely lost. If the linkage and motion were connected, if the wheels were not jacked-up, if there was enough steam to get them started, if the fire had not fallen too low . . . ? A hell of a lot of 'ifs', but at least there was a chance.

'No, it's not all I can do, so come on, darling.' He started to run back towards the station. 'Forget about calling the police, because with just a bit of luck we can stop those maniacs ourselves.'

'*Cambrian Rose*, Port Olwyn Locomotive Works 1872.' The engine shed was brightly lit and high above them the nameplate glinted like a mocking eye. As Boris had once told George, the old 2-4-0 looked raffish and not at all respectable: a lady of the town dressed up to kill and very gay in her apple-green livery piped with scarlet, her polished brasswork and steel couplings shining through the grease. The locomotive was also much bigger than the photograph had suggested. The immensely tall funnel and bulbous steam dome almost touched the roof of the shed and a tank engine parked alongside was dwarfed by her tender.

'Boris, you must be out of your mind.' Ruth watched him walk slowly round the chassis, and the very bulk of *Cambrian Rose* awed her. She had not heard his last sentence when they started to run back to the station and imagined he intended to try and reconnect the telephone wires. 'You don't honestly think you can catch up with George's car in that museum piece?'

'I think there is a possibility.' He concentrated on his inspection. The motion was coupled, steam was hissing flabbily from the valves and the wheels were free. The Westinghouse pump was disconnected which meant that the main brakes were out of action, but with no load behind the tender the hand brake would suffice.

'The only possibility is a horrible accident.' Ruth saw that a workbench was littered with tools and spare parts and she tugged at his jacket. 'Didn't you see the oil on George's hands? He must have been working on the thing when his father arrived and it's probably a death trap. How do you know that it'll hold the rails or the boiler won't burst if you get started? You saw how steep the descent is, so what happens if the brakes aren't working?'

'I don't know, darling, and the main brakes are not even con-nected. But I want her to go – not stop.' He lifted a wrench from the rear buffer bar and laid it beside the other tools. 'This is the only way we can put an end to George and Harry's blood bath and I've got to take it.'

'For God's sake come to your senses and grow up, Boris. Even if you can get this contraption to work what good are you going to do? Those madmen have a revolver and it's not our job to arrest them, so please let's go back to the car and change the wheel.' He had craned down beneath the tender and the engine and she knelt beside him.

'We'll get in touch with the police and they'll be caught before any more murders are committed. Our only responsibility is to report what has happened and we must consider ourselves a little. You've got the letter in your pocket and Grant is dead. You're completely safe at last, Boris, so think of us; of you and me. You said you loved me and that you wanted children. Well, I can give you children, darling, but not if I'm crushed under an engine.'

'I do love you, Ruth, I do want children from you, but there'll be plenty of time to play house.' Boris had checked the tender coupling and he pulled the envelope containing Grant's cheque from his pocket. 'If I can get this old girl to start, I'm hoping to try to stop George and Alban, but just in case anything goes wrong you'd better take this now.' He handed her the envelope and climbed up into the cab, knowing quite well that Ruth was correct. There was no need for him to produce any heroics. His only duty was to change a car wheel and inform the police. If he did that and forgot the locomotive, the future was secure.

Steam pressure, sixteen pounds; water level, satisfactory; brake pressure, nil. Boyhood journeys with his father came back to him while he inspected the gauges, and Boris realized that he was not being heroic at all. He had to try to stop the killers, but he was also bewitched by the thought of mastering *Cambrian Rose*.

'All right, you win Boris. I'll play hero with you, but remember you promised to play house afterwards.' Ruth pulled herself up beside him. 'Is there anything I can do to help?'

'Yes, you can act as stoker.' He opened the furnace door. The fire was banked high and the dampers were closed. The crust looked black and lifeless, but he could feel a surge of heat beneath it. 'Take that rod and try to break up the coals.' He nodded towards a pricker bar and continued his inspection of the cab. The main controls were on the opposite side to those of Russian locomotives, but the general layout was simple and should present few problems. That was the regulator handle on the far right, that was the reversing gear, those should be the blower screw and the ejector valves.

But only sixteen pounds' pressure and the line passed through the station up a pretty steep incline. Even without a load they'd be lucky to get away with that amount of steam in the boiler. He opened the screw to bring the blower into operation and squinted at the fire again.

'Good girl.' Ruth had been stabbing at the coals and little spurts were appearing through the inert mass like miniature volcanoes. Boris slammed the door shut and adjusted the dampers.

'Now release the tender brake; that wheel behind you, and keep your fingers crossed.' He moved the gear lever into forward position and raised the regulator.

'S . . . sh . . . shun . . .' The whisper was faint and hesitant and at first Boris felt sure that the steam pressure could never defeat the gradient. 'Shun . . . cha . . .' That was better. The exhaust note was still hesitant, but the pistons were moving, the connecting rods were bearing against the wheels, and *Cambrian Rose* was inching her seventy tons towards the station.

'Shun . . . cha . . . shun . . .' Boris looked at his watch. The platform was crawling alongside with agonizing slowness and George and his brother had a long start on them. If the car passed the crossing before the viaduct ahead of them he would have done nothing except waste time.

'Sha . . . shun . . . chansha . . .' That was much better. With every stride of the pistons, every revolution of the wheels, the blower was increasing the draught and the fire was burning brighter.

'Chansha . . . chanshun . . .' Much, much better. The platforms were behind them and the exhaust notes were growing stronger as they lumbered up through Bryncir village. George Grant might be a psychopath, but he was obviously an efficient mechanic and the locomotive was settling down to her work. The pressure gauge recorded thirty pounds when the last of the ruins fell away and its needle was rising steadily. In front of them lay the saucer-shaped tableland and beyond that the line stretched downhill almost all the way to Port Olwyn.

Keeping his hand on the regulator Boris leaned out of the cab to study the terrain. Though George had a good start, his passion for archaic machinery was against him. The shooting brake was a twenty-year-old Morris with a heavy body and a small engine and the road was poor. Where speed was concerned the locomotive might be the better vehicle and with luck George and his brother would find the road blocked by *Cambrian Rose* stationed on the open crossing at the head of the viaduct. During the drive up Boris had noticed a farmhouse less than half a mile from there. A red-hot pricker bar would effectively penetrate a car's radiator and also hold off its occupants till Ruth brought help. There might be two bullets left in Grant's revolver, but George and Alban would not waste them on him. Those bullets were for their own use; guarantees against captivity.

'Shacha . . . shesha . . . shunsha . . .' Everything depended on the old engine behaving herself and she was certainly doing so at the moment. The exhaust notes were rising steadily, steam pressure was approaching the hundred mark and the clank of the wheels was becoming a clattering roar. Boris shut off the blower and crossed to the furnace. Ruth was right about the possibility of a boiler explosion. George must have been testing the tubes when his father arrived, and if they blew, he and Ruth would be dead before they even heard the explosion.

Not only George; Harry Alban's hands had been oily, as well. Boris experienced a twinge of pity as he imagined the two brothers working happily away on the engine like children with a toy. Paddy Reilly and Ernest Grant had produced monsters; crazed animals that had to be destroyed or locked away, but there was still something terribly pathetic about their sickness and he could not help feeling compassion for them.

Compassion? That was a fine word for an M.V.D. operator to use. Boris opened the furnace door and laid the pricker bar amongst the white-hot coals. Pity and mercy were qualities he had been trained to discard, and he realized how very thorough his training had been. Yesterday, blurting out his shame to Ruth he had believed that he had changed, but had he deceived himself? Less than an hour ago he could have killed Sir Ernest Grant and his sole emotion would have been relief.

Boris leaned out of the cab again and eased back the regulator. The tableland had started to slope and the long descent lay before him. Speed was increasing alarmingly and they were bound to reach the crossing in good time unless a derailment or a mechanical failure took place. His eyes swept the moonlit hillside hoping to catch a glimpse of headlamps, but there was nothing to be seen.

'Ruth, I'll be stopping on the crossing soon and you'll see a farmhouse to the right. Once we've pulled up I want you to run to the farm and bring back all the help you can; tell the men to have dogs and shotguns with them.' He pushed past her and screwed down the tender brake, because the descent had started with a vengeance and whatever happened he must not overrun the crossing. 'And please don't argue with me, darling. Once it's safe to jump off the footplate don't wait for me; just run as hard as you can.'

That was better. The tender was slowing the engine and sparks were flying from its locked wheels. In front lay a cutting and a short tunnel and after that the level crossing, the tiny station and the viaduct. Boris reached over for the regulator and then threw himself back and released the brake. The road ahead was in view and car lights were moving down towards the crossing. George had made better time than he had imagined possible and it would be touch and go. He opened the regulator to its full travel and prayed for steam.

'TUNNEL AHEAD' . . . 'WHISTLE' . . . 'MAX SPEED 30 MPH'. The signs slid past and *Cambrian Rose* hurled herself forward. The open furnace door had damped the fire slightly, but the pressure gauge still registered ninety pounds and the incline was behind her. The walls of the crossing flew past and the tunnel loomed up to swallow them; its arch looking far too low for the chimney to clear. Blackness closed in, the roar of the wheels and the pounding pistons drove out thought and then there was light again. The tall viaduct stood silver-grey under the moon, they saw the glint of the cattle grids which flanked the crossing, another speed reduction sign, and another gleam of light that told Boris and Ruth that they had failed. The lights in front of them were red; the shooting brake was over the crossing and they were too late.

Too late, but also too fast. Boris slammed the regulator shut. He knew that the viaduct curved, but from the road he had not seen that the curve was so sharp and so sudden. They were approaching it at over fifty; the main brakes were out of action and the tender could never slow the engine in time. Unless he could reduce speed quickly the wheels were bound to jump the rails and plunge over the viaduct. He shouted at Ruth to brace herself and threw the gear lever into reverse.

It was as though they had met a cliff face. The boiler seemed to rear up in front of him, the cab shuddered and lurched madly and the piston beats became a howl of protesting metal; so loud that he never heard Ruth scream. Her body had been jerked forward by the arrested motion and before he saw her she was swinging out towards the edge of the viaduct.

'Got you. It's all right. I've got you.' He had caught her arm, but the footplate was still lurching violently while the wheels skidded on the track, and he fell to his knees. Unless he could grasp something solid they would be pulled out together. His left hand flailed out in desperation as he slid across the platform and finally closed on an object that made his own screams join Ruth's. A searing instrument of torture that caused him more pain than he imagined could exist. But at least it was a solid object and with his

fingers clutching the edge of the red-hot furnace door he hauled
Ruth back into the cab.

'That lever . . . pull it down.' He lay gasping on the floor and
nodded towards the regulator. With the steam valves in reverse
the locomotive had started to lumber backwards. 'Now, put the
lower lever in mid position and then screw down the tender brake.
Good.'

The engine's safety was taken care of and he could inspect the
ruin of his hand. It looked exactly like fried bacon, the palm was
split wide open and the finger bones were protruding through the
shredded flesh.

'See what you can do for me now, Ruth.' She was rummaging
in the tool locker and he dragged himself to his feet fighting back
the urge to vomit. He felt almost as sick with emotion as physical agony, because once again he had failed. Thirty-two people
had died on the airliner because the hijackers had caught him off
guard. Now, two multiple killers had got clean away because he
had misjudged time and distance and slackened speed too early.
Soon the car would join the traffic on the main roads and George
and Harry could go where they pleased. Soon innocent women
would die and all because of him. There was only one more
crossing before the road junction at Port Olwyn and it was gated
up for the winter. Even if the gates were open and they could catch
up with the shooting brake, what good would it do? A cripple and
a girl were no match for two homicidal maniacs.

Could he possibly ram the car on the crossing? No, though the
buffer bar would break through the gates easily, it was too much
to expect that the locomotive and the car would reach the crossing
at the same time. So much to think about . . . so many factors to
consider. Ruth had found what she needed now and he held out his
hand to her, struggling to ignore pain and concentrate.

Yes, there was still a chance, though a pitifully small one.
The front wheels had been starting to leave the rails just before
he reversed the engine; he was quite sure of that, and after the
causeway he had seen a severe speed restriction sign and a very
sharp bend. Beyond that bend the railway track and the road ran
parallel along the causeway to Port Olwyn.

A very tiny chance, indeed, but though the attempt would certainly maim and possibly kill him it had to be taken. Sir Ernest Grant had run away from life but he had paid a debt before he died. Grant's death and the letter in his pocket gave him security, but not self-respect and he had his own account to settle.

Ruth had bandaged his hand with cotton waste and a handkerchief and Boris pulled out the envelope and examined its contents. Grant had not been nervous when he wrote the letter and the four lines of manuscript were as even and well constructed as print.

Dear Mr Tchagin,
   I am writing to inform you that Boris Stephanovich Dubassof, a man whom you believe to be dead, is, in fact, very much alive and working for my organization under the alias of Orel.

Boris threw the letter into the furnace. The paper flared before even touching the coals and he was free to live as he pleased, but in the glow of the fire he suddenly saw the verse from 'A Shropshire Lad', twisting before his eyes.

> Oh soon, and better so than later
> After long disgrace and scorn,
> You shot dead the household traitor,
> The soul that should not have been born.

That applied to George Grant and Harry Alban. It had applied to Ernest Grant with his megalomania and also to Paddy Reilly who had tortured children to revenge herself on their father. But didn't it apply to him as well? Hadn't his training and the things he had been forced to do made him a pariah? They were all corrupt, all traitors to life and the only difference was that he had a chance to make amends.

'Don't just stand there, Ruth.' He made himself sound impatient and angry. 'Run to that farm, as I said and for God's sake hurry. You must telephone the police.'

'I'm waiting for you, Boris.' She reached out to help him from the cab. 'That hand will go septic if you don't have it seen to soon, so come on, darling. The engine is useless to us now.'

'I said get going, Ruth. And please don't argue, because there's no time left and I'm too bloody tired to argue. Just do what I say for once.' He saw the refusal in her face and his right fist shot out.

'Sorry about that, my darling, but you may be grateful to me one day.' Boris's voice was very gentle as he lowered her unconscious body on to the ground and then he climbed back into the cab and made his preparations. With only one hand it took him all his strength to build up the fire and release the tender brake, but finally he was ready. *Cambrian Rose* snorted and rumbled off on her last journey.

This time there was going to be no mistake and no failure. While the locomotive drifted through the fells, he felt light-hearted and strangely elated and pain had ceased to trouble him. His burned hand somehow felt as though it were no longer a part of his own body.

'More draught, would you advise, Stephan Feodorovich?' He spoke aloud while he adjusted the dampers and checked the water level and the memory of his father gave him confidence. The fire was drawing well, steam was building up again and only one thing could hold him back. He had a lot of innocent blood on his conscience already and there must be no more. If there was any traffic on the causeway, a bus, a car, or even a solitary cyclist or pedestrian he would have to abandon the attempt and stop the engine before the crossing.

What were George and Harry doing at this moment, he wondered? Were they talking together and discussing their future plans, or was speech unnecessary? Had their private hell bound them so closely together that they could communicate without words? Above all how would George react when he saw the locomotive converging on the road? Would he put on speed or turn round and go back the way he had come? Most probably the former. George could hardly envisage his intentions and would suppose that he and Ruth were on their way to Port Olwyn to fetch help and would stop at the crossing gates.

Boris had no animosity towards the men he hoped to kill or

mutilate, but a deep clinical curiosity such as a scientist might feel for some virulent species of bacterium. Ernest Grant and Miss Reilly must have been blood relations, he supposed. Had that drawn them together in the first place and was it heredity or environment that had produced their children's mania? Probably a mixture of both, but whatever the truth might be, their union had borne bitter fruit which had to be destroyed.

There was the coast in sight at last. The line had dipped for a few hundred yards and then climbed over a bluff and he could see the lights of Port Olwyn, the line of the causeway and yachts riding at anchor in the bay beyond it. The headlamps of George's Morris were circling along the hills towards the crossing, but though the car had farther to go, Boris eased back the regulator. If he kept well in the rear till the last possible moment George and Alban might not see him before it was too late. He studied the terrain spread out before him, calculating the distances and the steepness of the incline.

'Cha . . . cha . . . rah . . .' Slowly and steadily the connecting rods strode on to the place of meeting: the bend before the sea wall where the road and the railway joined and crossed the estuary side by side. Boris glanced at the gauges and prayed that the causeway would be free of traffic, and he heard dogs bark as he passed a cluster of farm buildings and saw a woman staring incredulously at the engine from a lighted window. Was she a small, neat, middle-aged woman who resembled Paddy Reilly, he wondered? Was she a potential victim of the madmen in front of him?

'Three miles for them, two miles for us, my lovely Welsh girl.' Boris gave the pressure gauge an affectionate pat and opened the blower screw. He must only increase speed very slightly, but have a full head of steam ready for the final effort.

'Cha . . . rah . . . tah . . . our mighty Russian nation . . . Soviet land, so beautiful and free . . .' The words of a Red Army song joined the exhaust note while he leaned out of the cab and watched the road and the railway track starting to converge. The shooting brake had just passed the last tiny hamlet before the crossing and the viaduct was almost straight below him. In the moonlight he could see just how sharp the bend was and he remembered that there had been a ten-mile-an-hour speed restriction notice. When he reversed on the viaduct the engine had been travelling at about sixty miles an hour and he was certain that she would have left the rails if he had not stopped her in time. The curve ahead was much more severe and fifty should be adequate to derail the wheels. Provided the road was clear, he would jump just before the crossing and escape with a few broken bones and bruises. A small price to pay for self-respect and the end of the Hangman.

They still had not seen him. The shooting brake was no more than a mile from the crossing and travelling fairly slowly. George and his brother believed they were safe and he could picture their faces as they thought about the future. The roads from Port Olwyn and the big cities where men could go unnoticed and women who reminded them of Paddy Reilly were to be found. They knew that final defeat was inevitable; two bullets had been hoarded as a guarantee against capture, but before Ernest Grant's revolver gave his sons peace, the witch hunt would continue.

Three-quarters of a mile . . . half a mile. The Morris was roughly the same distance as himself from the crossing and the road along the causeway was clear of traffic.

At last they had spotted him. Yes, the car had increased speed but George was not flogging her. The ancient vehicle would be difficult to handle on the winding road and they could not have guessed his intentions. Probably George and Alban imagined that he would stop at the crossing gates and run for help. That would not worry the brothers greatly. Before he reached the police station they would be far away.

A third of a mile. He had done all that was possible and could think about himself. Boris threw the regulator handle into its highest notch and craned out of the cab. The verge was grass and he had a fair chance of survival.

'Off you go, *Rose.*' He gave the pressure gauge a final pat, but the encouragement was not needed. With the slope to help her and a hundred and ten pounds against the piston heads, the 2-4-0 surged forward and his work was finished. He grasped the rail of the tender and prepared to spring to safety.

'Stay where you are, Boris Dubassof.' The words snapped at his ears and he swung round to see that he was not alone. A man was standing by the opposite window and though his face was in shadow, Boris recognized that voice. He must have heard its orders a hundred times in the past. Peter Vanin was dead, but he had come back to join him on the footplate.

'To be free of your debts, you must pay them in full, Boris, so don't gamble. What will happen if you jump and the locomotive manages to remain on the rails?'

'I will have achieved nothing, Peter.' The car swung over the crossing and for a single second Vanin's face was lit up by the head-lights and Boris saw his features clearly. 'Those men will go free and it might be a long time before I could tell the police anything.'

'Exactly, Boris, so do not take chances. Stay where you are till I give you the order to jump.'

The image blurred and vanished, but Boris still stood on the footplate with his hand grasping the rail of the tender and his eyes fixed on the crossing gates hurtling towards him. If the wheels did remain on the track after he had jumped he would have failed completely so he had to wait for Vanin's final order. But no order came. All he heard was the crash of woodwork and then the floor of the cab lurched sideways and threw him out into the night.

The locomotive was thirty yards behind the car when she reached the crossing, her speed was over sixty miles an hour, and the gates did nothing to slow her progress. The buffer-beam burst through them, and though the wheels ploughed wildly over the shattered timbers they held the track and she roared on with steam bellowing through the safety valves.

But the wheels could not hold the bend. For a brief instant their flanges clawed at the rails, then they left them and she tore straight on towards the edge of the embankment. A seventy-ton Jugger-naut: an avalanche of metal, coal and water that shot into the air and went plunging down to engulf the shooting brake.

Cambrian Rose had been one of the passions of George Grant's life and death did not separate him from her. Joined together as one mass, locomotive and car continued in unison along the road till the boiler met the sea wall and exploded.

Postscript

High up on the hillside Ruth had come to and started to stagger towards the farm. The wind was blowing directly from the sea and she heard the thunder of the explosion. Later on she heard sirens, but she was still too dazed to take in what the noises meant. All she could think about was Boris. She loved him, she had wanted to stay with him, but he had rejected her help and struck her.

Almost blind with tears Ruth toiled up the track to the farm. Boris had thought she had realized what his plans were, but he had been wrong. She had no idea how he intended to destroy George and his brother, and their fate seemed unimportant to her now. The only thing she wanted to know was why he had rejected her and what had happened to him.

She had to wait a long time for the answers. Twenty-four hours passed before he opened his eyes in the hospital and three days before he was strong enough to tell her himself.

ALSO AVAILABLE FROM VALANCOURT BOOKS